HER GRUFF BOSS

Amelia Smarts

Copyright © 2023 Amelia Smarts

No part of this book may be reproduced or transmitted in any form or by any means, electronic or mechanical, including photocopying, recording, or by any information storage and retrieval system, without permission in writing from the publisher.

Published by Amelia Smarts
ameliasmarts.com

Smarts, Amelia
Her Gruff Boss
ISBN 9798385946020

Cover Design by Designrans
Image by Period Images

All rights reserved.

This book is intended for adults only. Spanking and sexual activities represented in this book are fantasies only, intended for adults. Nothing in this book should be interpreted as the author's advocating any nonconsensual spanking activity or the spanking of minors.

CHAPTER ONE

Texas, 1892

Carter opened the door to find Anna Brown standing on his doorstep holding a basket of eggs. She looked taller than he remembered, but he was foggy about the last time he'd seen her. She was undoubtedly at the funeral a couple of weeks prior, but all he could remember from the service were the purple flowers around the preacher's pulpit and the gray pallor of his wife's coffin.

"My ma thought you could use some eggs, since you gave up chickens for cows," Anna said, handing him the basket.

Carter took it and waved for her to follow as he walked to the kitchen. Some years back, he had sold his chickens—most to Anna's family—and since then had focused solely on herding cows and training horses. A couple of months ago he'd considered building a small coop to house hens so his family would have a fresh supply of eggs every day. Then Nalin had fallen ill, and his grand plans had faded along with her.

There had been a steady stream of visitors to his cabin since the funeral. Some brought casseroles and cooked beans. Others brought sugar, flour, and eggs. That's what people did, he discovered, when a man's wife died. They brought food. Earlier that day, a generous neighbor had dropped off a newly slaughtered and plucked chicken, which he'd just removed from the keep to cook when he'd heard Anna's quiet knock.

"I don't suppose you drink coffee," Carter said to her as an invitation as he regarded her appearance. She was at least seventeen according to his calculations and not at all dressed or styled to attract a suitor like most girls her age. Two long braids laid on top of her chest, which made her appear younger than she was. She wore a style of dress more appropriate for a younger girl too. It was all ribbon and cotton, and it shone a cheerful yellow color that belied her somber expression.

"I'll have some milk if you have it."

Carter poured milk into a tin cup and handed it to her. Anna drank thirstily and looked around. He looked with her to see what she saw. The main room of the cabin was messy. He'd been sleeping fitfully on the sofa, which was apparent because of the wrinkled quilt strewn across it. In the armchair was a pile of clothes that needed to be washed. Dirty dishes sat stacked on the kitchen counter, and a thin layer of dust covered every surface, including the hardwood floor. The room was dark and stuffy because Carter hadn't opened the windows despite the pleasant spring weather. He was sure it stank to high heaven of tobacco and dirty dishes, though he couldn't know. All of his senses had become dull.

"Mr. Barnes, there's another reason besides bringing you eggs that I came over."

Carter sat on a stool at the kitchen table. He lit his pipe and looked at her, waiting for her to continue. Anna shifted for a moment under his gaze and then sat down on the stool next to him. She folded her hands in front of her.

"The thing is I'm not too interested in school. I quit a year ago because I know how to write and do some math and I don't see any other reason for being there. My pa agreed that I could stay home and work around the farm. He says that I'm real good at practical things and that not everyone is cut out for book learning."

"True enough," Carter said. He wasn't sure what point she was making. He took a puff from his pipe. He had never liked school much himself, preferring to be outdoors rounding cows and training horses from a young age. As his parents' only child, he'd inherited his ranch. It ran parallel to the Rem River, which made the land lush and profitable. The town of Porter bustled two miles west and boasted a supply store, meatpacking shop, and blacksmith, all of which were necessary for Carter to be as successful as he was.

Patrick—nicknamed Paddy by his mother the day he was born—toddled out from the bedroom, rubbing his eyes and mumbling about milk. Carter stood and poured a second cup, half as full as Anna's. He lifted his son to a free stool at the table. "Sit here and try not to spill it."

Paddy drank from the cup haphazardly. Imprints from a pillow lined his flushed cheeks, and sweat pasted his tangled, dark hair to his forehead.

Carter sat back down on his stool and returned his attention to Anna, who was observing with a look of doubt the child's attempt to drink from the cup. Looking to Carter, she said, "I'd like to work for you. I can watch over Paddy. He can't be more than three years old and you can't take him along with you to the range or send him to school yet." She looked around the cabin again and added, "Plus I can cook and clean. Like I said, I'm good at practical things."

When he didn't respond, she stood and walked to the counter. "Like this chicken. I can cook it today for your supper."

For the thousandth time, Carter silently cursed the heavens for taking his wife from him. He didn't want to have this conversation. He and his son had been surviving off the generosity of neighbors since his wife's death, during which time he'd been dimly aware that someone would need to mind Paddy when he returned to overseeing the ranch. His foreman, Ben, had taken over Carter's duties for the time being. It had crossed his mind that he might ask the foreman's wife, Grace, to care for his son, but he hadn't made a point of asking her yet.

Finding someone to cook and clean hadn't been in his thoughts at all, but he never would have considered Anna if it had been. Because of his friendship with her parents, he had watched her grow up, was fond of her even, but he didn't have patience for folly when it came to his household and business, and folly generally accompanied youth. Then again, he thought, not everyone was thoughtless and unfocused at that time in their lives. When he was her age twelve years back, he'd dedicated his serious attention to building a business.

"You want to work here instead of getting a job in town or going out with your friends?" he asked doubtfully.

Paddy banged the almost-empty cup down on the table, splashing drops of milk on his face.

Carter grabbed the cup out of his son's chubby hands and lowered him to the ground, then rested an elbow on the table and took another puff from his pipe.

"Yes, sir, I'd really like working here. I'd rather work here for some money than work at the farm for nothing."

She was good at arguing her case, Carter thought. He focused a stern gaze on her and considered it. He employed more than a dozen men at the ranch, but he had never employed a woman. It was hard for him to wrap his head around hiring her for more than just that reason. To him, she was still a child. He remembered when her parents had moved from Maryland to Texas with Anna and her sisters some ten years back and settled the sprawling land next to his ranch.

Carter was a newly married man just twenty years old when he first met Anna and her family. He had a distinct memory of rescuing the eight-year-old girl from a tree she'd climbed. His wife had discovered her.

※ ※ ※

"Anna Brown, what the devil are you doing up there?" Nalin called.

"I can't get down. Please can you help me, Mrs. Barnes?"

"Don't you know you shouldn't climb that high if you can't get back down?" Nalin scolded.

Carter sneaked up behind his new bride and wrapped his arms around her, causing her to emit a startled squeak. Carter followed Nalin's gaze upward to the little girl in the tree. "Sakes alive, what do we have here?" he asked, releasing Nalin and holding his hand over his forehead to block the sun.

"Anna's gone and gotten herself stuck in the tree. She doesn't reckon she can climb down,"

Nalin said. Her voice was edged with fear. Though she acted annoyed, Carter knew her primary feeling was concern.

Anna had fastened her arms and legs around a strong horizontal limb. She let out a pitiful whimper.

Carted said, "I'll come up and get you, Anna. Hang tight and don't fuss." He removed his slicker and handed it to Nalin. As he climbed the tree, limb by limb, he realized this was the second time Anna had managed to get herself into trouble within the span of two days. He planned to give her a good scolding as soon as he got her down from the tree, and that plan was firmly in place until he climbed up high enough to see her face. It was dirty and streaked with tears. Her big green eyes held terror. She'd torn her dress and skinned her knees.

Carter lifted her in to his chest, and she wrapped her arms and legs around him. "All right, little lady. Let's get your feet back on the ground. I've got to use my hands for getting down out of here, not for holding you, so you hang on tight to me, you hear?"

"I will," she said, and clung to him tighter.

"Careful! Take it slow," Nalin called up to him.

He groaned. "You don't say, Nalin? You don't think maybe I should speed things up and jump down from here?"

Anna giggled.

Nalin called up, "Don't be a dunce, Carter.

I'm warning you, I'm plumb out of patience."

"All right, all right. Criminy." He moved to a lower branch. To Anna, he said, "You'd be in a peck of trouble with that sage hen if I wasn't here. She's not in a good mood. Lucky for you, I know how to ruffle her feathers. She'll forget all about you and take her licks to me."

"I'm sorry," Anna said earnestly. "Will you be all right?"

Carter chuckled. "I'll live."

When they arrived on the ground, Carter set Anna on her feet. "There you go, little lady. Scoot back to the cabin and get cleaned up. And get a wiggle on." He gave her behind a smack before she ran off.

Turning to face Nalin's scowl, he said, "Where's my kiss for that heroic rescue?"

Nalin huffed. "You were way too easy on that child. She could have been seriously hurt or killed, and you acted like it was a game."

"What would you have me do? Give her a hiding?"

"No, of course not. But you could at least explain to her the danger."

"You didn't see her face up there. Trust me, she knew she was in danger. I think she probably likes a little danger and that's what got her there in the first place." Carter took Nalin into his arms. "Enough of your carping, wife. Give me a kiss before I steal one from you."

"You're impossible," she said, melting into

his arms before she kissed him.

* * *

Carter puffed on his pipe. How fast life could change. In what seemed a flash, his wife was dead and Anna was no longer a child.

"Does your pa know you're here asking to work?" Carter asked.

Anna nodded. "Yes, sir. He said I would be lucky to work for you."

After another moment of mulling, he agreed. "We can give it a try. Fifty cents a day sound fair?"

She smiled. "I'll start today."

"Tomorrow," he said, suddenly weary and ready for her to leave. He didn't want to pretend to be sociable. It drained him of his limited energy.

"I'll be back tomorrow at dawn. Thank you, Mr. Barnes."

"See you then," he said, rising and walking her to the door.

"Bye-bye, Paddy." Anna waved to the child and stepped out.

CHAPTER TWO

The next morning, Anna walked the mile down the path to Carter's house. She planned to first open every window to air out the stuffiness. She would bake bread and play with Paddy. She was excited about her new job.

She thought about Carter. She had always liked him and knew he was a kind man beneath his brusque exterior. She'd heard stories about how he ran his ranch. He paid his men fairly, but wouldn't hesitate to fire someone who wasn't up to snuff. Anna's father had told her that the worst thing someone could do under his employ was mistreat one of his animals. Paul once witnessed Carter wrestle a horsewhip from a cowhand who was beating a horse and take it to him. Carter got in two lashes before the cowhand escaped to safety. Those kinds of incidences made Carter feared and respected by his employees, and Anna already felt the same. His hard jaw and stern eyes made him intimidating, but she knew he had a gentler, teasing side that had made her laugh as a child. She also understood his compassion for animals, since she possessed that as well. She couldn't bear to see a living creature suffer.

When she arrived at the cabin and lifted her hand to knock, Carter opened the door before she could. He was carrying Paddy, who looked grumpy. The child wore pants but no shirt. "I haven't fed him yet," Carter said. "Will you make us some breakfast?"

"Of course," Anna said, entering and getting to work in the kitchen while Carter sat on the sofa with the child. She found the bacon and butter, lit a fire adeptly, and retrieved the frying pan that hung by the stove. After frying the bacon, she scrambled eggs and sliced cheese. Carter had already made the coffee.

Paddy fussed and Carter bounced him on his knee. That did nothing to quiet the child. His fussing turned into cries and then a tantrum. Carter set Paddy on the ground, where he arched his back and pounded his fist into the floor.

Carter eyed him with resignation. "What's wrong, little man?"

Paddy answered his question with a long wail. Soothing the child was probably up to Nalin when she was alive, Anna thought. And now up to her, she realized suddenly. She piled food on a plate and set it on the table. She wrestled Paddy off the floor into her arms, sat on a stool in the kitchen, and set him on her lap. She planted him high on her legs against her stomach where she could firmly hug him to her and prevent him from arching out of her hold. She reached for a piece of bacon.

"Are you hungry, sweetheart? Do you like bacon?"

"Yes," he cried but still squirmed, unconvinced that bacon warranted calming down.

"You can have as much bacon as you want. Take it, baby." She held the bacon in front of him. Paddy took it in his hand and squirmed a bit less.

"What about eggs? Do you like eggs?'

Paddy settled. His cries receded into hiccups. "Yes," he said, his voice trembling. "I like eggs." He bit into the bacon.

"You can have as many eggs as you want too, all right?"

"All right," Paddy said, his voice still aggrieved.

"What else do you like, sweetie?"

Paddy tilted his face up and stared with curious, wet eyes at her. "I like candy."

"Me too," Anna exclaimed. "I love candy, and I have some at home. I will bring it for you tomorrow."

Paddy looked pleased with that news. He took another piece of bacon from the plate in front of him. Anna could smell Paddy's dirty hair because it was right below her nose. The odor was strong and sour, and she wondered how long it had been since his last bath. Carter didn't look too clean either. He had a thick head of what was usually handsome dark hair, but it was oily and dented in the places where his Stetson had made impressions. His hands and shirt were tidy enough, but dust and crusted mud streaked his denim trousers all the way down the front and back.

Carter ate slowly, occasionally looking up to glance at Paddy in Anna's lap. Near the end of the meal, he asked Anna in a rough tone, "Why haven't you eaten?"

Anna hadn't been sure whether she should eat his food while there, but his question made her realize she could. "I'll eat when you both finish. Thank you, Mr. Barnes."

After his last bite, Carter stood and moved to the living area, where he picked up his boots by the door. Anna watched him discreetly. When she was a child, she thought he was a giant, and he still seemed like one to her, though now she was only a few inches shorter. He was hard from his face to his feet. The belt around his trousers was linked by a metal buckle etched with a bucking stallion, but that was the only ornament. His shirt was plain white with sleeves to his wrists. It buttoned down the front. Carter pushed some clothes off the armchair so he could sit down. He wrestled his boots onto his feet. She noticed that the boots didn't have spurs on them.

Leaning over, he rummaged through the clothes he'd pushed to the floor and found his riding gloves, which he tucked halfway in his back pocket upon standing. He walked to the bedroom, his steps thunderous now that he tread with boots on the hardwood floor. He returned a few moments later wearing his tan hat.

"Pa pa pa pa. Where you going, Pa?" babbled Paddy, happy now that he was no longer hungry.

Carter didn't answer his question. "You be good, Patrick."

Anna thought Carter might instruct her on what to do while he was away, or at least let her know when he'd be back, but he said nothing to her and strode out the door.

Nine hours passed before she saw Carter again. During that time, Anna worked nonstop. She opened the windows. She boiled water and soaked the dirty dishes before scouring them clean. She washed the clothes on the floor next to the armchair, which included two pairs of Carter's trousers that were dirtier than those he wore. She baked bread, bathed Paddy, swept the hardwood floor, and roasted a chicken. Carter arrived home to a cleaner cabin and a hot meal. Anna felt weary after the long day attending to domestic duties, but she knew that not every day would be so hard. If she worked smart, she'd be able to bring the household up to acceptable living conditions within a few days. Then her work would just be maintenance.

Carter picked up Paddy and threw him in the air. The child enjoyed the attention and laughed, but Anna could tell that Carter wasn't feeling playful. His movements were stiff, and she reckoned he only played with his son to maintain some semblance of normalcy.

Anna placed food on the table, and the three of them sat down together for the second time that day. Conversation was not part of the meal since Carter didn't speak and Anna was used to taking speaking cues from her elders. When Carter and Nalin ate supper with her family when she was a child, she'd adhered to her parents' admonishment that children should be seen and not heard, and that dynamic between Carter and Anna remained in place that evening.

Paddy was under no such admonishment from his father to remain quiet. When he wasn't eating, he was talking. Sometimes he was doing both at the same time. "Miss Anna made a fire, Pa. I took a bath and played with the blocks."

Carter nodded and said *"mm hmm"* for his side of the conversation until Paddy said, "Where's my ma? I want Mama." His bottom lip quivered.

Anna's fork stopped on the way to her mouth. Carter didn't look up. He chewed and swallowed his bite of food and said quietly without showing emotion, "Mama's not here anymore, Patrick. She went to heaven."

The little boy's eyes filled with tears, but Anna managed to divert his attention to a piece of bread with butter before he began crying in earnest. Anna felt profound sadness, suddenly, sitting in this cabin. She felt like the weight of the sadness would suffocate her, and she longed to be outside away from this motherless boy and wifeless man.

Carter may have sensed her discomfort because he said, "It's late. I'll take you home in the buggy."

"Oh, don't bother, Mr. Barnes. I'll walk." She stood and set her plate on the counter. She would wash dishes tomorrow.

"No. It's almost dark."

Anna opened her mouth to protest again, but Carter held up a hand to stop her. "Look, I don't have the patience to argue with you. You're my responsibility. It's dark. I'm taking you home in the buggy, and I won't hear another word about it. Do I make myself clear?"

Anna looked down quickly, hoping he wouldn't catch the wounded expression on her face. She was only trying to make life easier for him, and he had gotten cross with her. "Yes, sir," she said to the floor. She walked outside to wait for him, closing the door behind her a little harder than she would have if she hadn't felt bruised.

Carter hooked one of his horses to the buggy and within fifteen minutes the three of them were on their way to her family's farm. Paddy sat between Carter and Anna. Shortly after they left, Paddy leaned over and fell asleep on Anna's lap.

"I'll pay you once a week on Saturday," Carter said. "Then you can take Sunday off."

"I can come Sunday too if you want. I don't go to church."

"No need."

Anna felt like she should explain what she had just confessed. "I don't like church. I don't think God listens to people."

Carter didn't say anything for what seemed like ages. Anna was afraid she'd revealed too much and Carter would fire her for being a heathen.

Instead he said, "No, I don't reckon he does either."

Anna felt sympathy for Carter then and longed to show him kindness. She hesitated for a moment but then reached over to touch his right hand, which was settled on his denim-clad thigh. "I'm sorry for your loss, Mr. Barnes."

Carter didn't move, and when he spoke, he wasn't exactly cold, but he wasn't warm either. "Thank you," was his reply.

Anna removed her hand and rested it on Paddy's sleeping head, worried that she had said something wrong. When they pulled up to the cabin, they found Anna's father Paul reclining on a chair on the porch. He wore farmer's overalls and a smile.

Carter stepped out of the buggy and held up his hand in an obligatory way to Anna. She carefully moved Paddy's head from her lap to the seat and clasped Carter's strong hand to steady her descent.

"Hello, cowboy," Paul said to Carter. "I hear

you're giving my girl a taste of the rancher's life."

Carter and Anna stepped up the porch stairs and Carter shook Paul's outstretched hand. Anna's mother, Margaret, joined them. "Carter," she exclaimed. "You can't imagine how pleased we are that you hired Anna. We know she'll be in good hands with you. Care for some apple pie? I baked it today."

"Thank you, Margie, but I'd best get my nipper to bed," he said, nodding his head toward the buggy. Paddy was still asleep. In another moment Carter had climbed back into his buggy.

Anna and her parents watched as it disappeared out of sight, into the night.

CHAPTER THREE

The following days at the cabin continued much like the first. The sadness was prevalent but unspoken. Carter rarely talked to Anna, not even to greet her when she arrived. She had to guess which domestic chores she should do since Carter never uttered a word of direction unless asked. He didn't like being asked. She learned that the hard way one morning as he was getting ready to leave.

Anna pointed to the holes in the shirt he was wearing. "Mr. Barnes, do you need me to mend your shirt? It's ripping at the seams."

Carter looked up briefly from his task of buckling his belt and responded gruffly, "Mend it tomorrow. Not that I can see how it matters, even a little bit, that there are holes in my work shirt."

"The holes will get bigger if they're not mended, that's all," she replied, her tone rueful.

Carter glowered at her. He untucked and unbuttoned the shirt, removed it, and tossed it in a wad on the armchair.

Anna watched him anxiously. Without his shirt he looked even fiercer. She hadn't thought that possible. His corded arms connected to broad, muscled shoulders. The skin on his chest was almost as dark as his tanned face, and an angry-looking scar slanted down the left side of his torso. Brown-black hair wisped around his chest, starting at his collarbone and trailing down, disappearing into his denims. He strode to the bedroom, emerged buttoning a shirt without holes, and headed for the front door. On his way, he slowed and his shoulders slouched. He put a palm on the doorframe and leaned his forehead into the crook of his elbow for a moment before he straightened and turned to Anna.

Rubbing a hand across his face, which was thick with stubble from not having shaved for what must have been at least a few days, he said, "Forgive my ill temper. You must understand it's not to do with you."

Anna's response was heartfelt. "I know, Mr. Barnes."

She did understand, but after that morning, Anna felt equally afraid of asking him questions and of doing something wrong. When she found a crate of canned goods buried in the cellar, she wasn't sure whether he was saving it. She considered it for a couple days, then decided to open a jar of peaches and make cobbler. Carter ate the pie that evening without a word, and she breathed a sigh of relief.

She felt greater trepidation when it came to Nalin's belongings. For weeks, Anna stepped over a pile of Nalin's clothes in the bedroom before finally washing and folding them away in the bottom drawer of the dresser. When Carter arrived home that day, she stood in the kitchen frozen with fear as he walked into his room. She didn't know how these things worked. Perhaps he wanted Nalin's clothes to be out on the floor. Anna recognized that they had made the room look like Nalin still lived in it. When Carter emerged from the bedroom, she searched his face. He wore the same stern, detached expression, so she relaxed.

Anna tried to guess Carter's favorite foods by the way that he ate, but she wasn't able to figure it out. Not a single look of pleasure crossed his face, regardless of what food she put in front of him. Anna was a good cook and tried without luck to tempt him to enjoy her pies, sweet bread, cakes, and various roast suppers. He ate whatever she put in front of him, but he never expressed enjoyment or appreciation. She didn't care about being thanked. What bothered her was feeling like nothing she did mattered. He never complained about anything she did, nor did he praise her.

She thought this was a good thing at first. At least he wasn't criticizing her or demanding that she bend to his wishes. But then she started to wish he would demand something. She would have welcomed any reaction that showed he was the slightest bit affected by what happened around him.

Their routine persisted for months. Anna showed up early. She spent the day at Carter's house cleaning, cooking, and minding Paddy while Carter worked. Carter returned in the late afternoon or evening. The three of them ate supper before she left. If they finished supper while there was still daylight and the weather was fair, she walked home. If it was raining or dark, Carter would drive her home in his buggy. She tried protesting once more that she could walk when it was dusk and not yet dark, but he gave her such a withering look that her stomach tightened into knots. She didn't suggest it again.

Paddy was as drawn to Anna as Carter was detached from her. Within a week of her working there, Paddy made it a habit to find his way to her lap whenever she sat down. He latched onto her skirt and followed her around while she did her chores. He asked questions about everything she did.

"Hush your yammering," Anna would say to him when she would tire of answering his questions. But the truth was she welcomed his little voice because the house would have been quieter than a prayer service without it. Sometimes out of the blue, Paddy's face would crumple and he would gaze at her. Anna thought that had something to do with him realizing she wasn't his ma. Whenever he looked at her like that,

Anna would scoop him into her arms and give him a kiss before finding something sweet for him to eat. She spent some of the money Carter paid her on candy from town. The candy was for her too, if she was honest with herself, but mostly it was for Paddy.

Carter caught her giving Paddy candy for the second time in one day. He said, "You'll spoil him, you know."

"He's not spoiled," she said with more force than she intended. "He's a good child, and it makes him happy."

Carter looked at her for several beats and then grunted. "Nalin used to say that. In the same outraged tone of voice, too." He shook the paper he was reading to straighten it. "Women," he muttered, sounding mildly exasperated.

Anna felt bad then and considered apologizing, but his nose was already back in the paper. Carter bought the Sunday paper in town weekly and spent a few minutes reading it every morning before he left for his work. He never read anything out loud, which bothered her. Her father and mother read articles aloud to get her and her sisters thinking about current events, and the whole family would discuss the happenings around town. Her pa sometimes asked Anna's opinion about the news, which made her feel important. Carter never asked her about anything. He didn't care about her opinion. He didn't care whether she was in the room or not. He didn't care what food she cooked or if she washed and mended his clothes. He didn't care if the house was clean or dirty. He didn't care about anything the earthly world had to offer.

Anna felt bold one day and decided to address him while he was reading the paper. "What's that article about, Mr. Barnes?"

He ignored her. He didn't look up or respond. It was as if she hadn't said a thing, and Anna stood there staring at the top of his bent head, growing irate. It was one thing for him not to speak to her, but for him to actually ignore her question was a snub she couldn't accept. She stormed to the kitchen and washed the dishes as loudly as she could, hoping it would ruin his concentration on whatever article he was reading that she was not to know about. Anna heard Carter sigh loudly after a minute of her banging silverware against the dishes.

"For crying out loud," he muttered.

Anna's back was turned to him and she smiled with smug satisfaction that she had managed to annoy him. Something snapped inside of her and she decided that she was going to break something of his. Maybe then he would have the decency to react, to show her some attention and emotion. No one had ignored her as Carter did or made her feel like everything she did was pointless. In school she had not been the best student. It was hard for her to concentrate on homework because she preferred to help with the animals at her family's farm. The schoolmarm had criticized her work and even rapped her knuckles a few times. That was preferable to being ignored.

Her ma praised her cooking. Her pa thanked her when she fed the chickens. Her sisters annoyed her and caused problems that now seemed refreshing. And here was Carter, for months her main source of grown-up companionship, and he wouldn't even answer a simple question. She knew he was grieving. She felt compassion for him, and she'd been able to understand and tolerate his stupor to a point, but she had finally reached the end of her patience.

She thought maybe the best thing would be to quit and walk out, but she didn't want to leave. Despite how much his apathy injured her, she craved his presence, and she felt excited hearing the sharp clicking of his horse's hooves when he returned to the cabin in the evenings. It didn't make sense to her that she wanted to be around him. She supposed she held out hope that the Carter she knew from her childhood still existed somewhere under the layers of sadness. The less he paid attention to her, the more she longed for him to notice her.

As she clattered dishes around, she decided a glass would be a good thing to break. She thought about how she would go about it. She didn't want to make it obvious that it was on purpose, so she settled on a plan to let it slip through her soapy fingers. That seemed the most likely way for it to happen by accident. Glancing back to find Carter still trying to read his paper, she soaped up her hands, picked up the glass she'd been drinking from, and let it fall. It shattered loudly into a thousand pieces on the hardwood floor. For a moment after, there was no sound.

Paddy broke the silence. "Uh oh!" he said. In his bare feet, he padded toward Anna and the glass.

"Patrick, come here," Carter said. The command halted Paddy's steps. Carter stood, folded his paper in half twice, and slapped it down on the table at the end of the sofa. The noise made Anna jump.

Paddy walked into Carter's open arms. Setting him on the sofa, Carter said, "You stay here while this gets cleaned up."

"All right, Pa," Paddy said.

Anna felt horrified as Carter approached her looking as tetchy as a teased snake. She couldn't believe what she had just done and regretted it the second after the glass hit the floor. She had never done anything so childish in her life, not even when she was an actual child! Her heartbeat quickened. Gone was the feeling of smugness at getting Carter back for ignoring her. She no longer wanted to see any kind of emotion or attention from him because she knew it would most likely be anger, and the thought of him angry frightened her. She desperately wished she could take it back.

"I-I'm so sorry," Anna said, her eyes not leaving his face.

Carter stopped when he reached the glass on the floor and surveyed it. Anna was thankful that for a short time the glass provided a barrier between him and her.

"You broke that on purpose." The accusation was leveled at her without the faintest trace of doubt.

Anna gulped air. She protested a little too strongly and in too much detail. "No! I didn't. It slipped out of my fingers because of the soap that is all over my hands from washing the dishes. See?" She held out her soapy hands as proof.

He scoffed. "You're a terrible liar."

Carter walked outside and returned with a broom and dustpan. He swept glass into a pile.

"I'll do that, Mr. Barnes," Anna said, feeling contrite.

Carter ignored her and continued to sweep. After he gathered most of the glass into one pile, he swept the shards into the pan and took it to the rubbish bin out front. Returning after what seemed to Anna like a very long time, he repeated his motions for the few remaining pieces of glass.

From where he was crouched at her feet sweeping the last of it into the pan, he said, "The article was about how sheepherders and cattle ranchers are scrapping over grasslands."

He rose in front of Anna to his full height. Anna prayed he would take it out of her pay and not out of her hide, but either or both seemed possible from the way he bore his eyes into hers. He studied her for a moment. Then, to her immense surprise and relief, his dark eyes softened and twinkled at her knowingly. He retreated, taking the last of the glass outside.

CHAPTER FOUR

Not a word about the glass incident was spoken in the weeks that followed. Their lives continued in the same quiet manner, but Anna noticed that Carter was more responsive to her than before. She still didn't dare ask him too many questions, but when she did, he would answer her, and not in an impatient manner like before.

During a vicious rainstorm, Anna arrived a few minutes past her usual time, drenched from head to toe. She walked in without knocking, which had become routine, and Carter looked up from the fireplace where he was adding a log from a crouched position.

Paddy ran to give her a hug, which she returned at a distance to avoid getting him too wet.

She felt like she should explain to Carter why she was there. "I thought the rain might clear up later and you'd want to go out. But then it started raining really hard halfway here. I suppose I should've stayed home."

"Yes, you should have," Carter said, his voice stern. "Come warm yourself."

Carter poked the log, causing sparks to fly. Anna rushed to the fireplace and stood next to him. She felt cold and awkward. She needed to get out of her clothes and into something dry but was unsure how to go about it. Carter finished positioning the logs and stood up.

When she saw his face, she lifted her eyebrows in surprise. He looked almost like a different person. He had bathed and combed his hair, but what stood out most was his smooth face. He had actually shaved properly, not just given his face a few hasty scrapes. She could smell the soap on his skin, and she felt drawn to him in a new way.

For a moment, he examined her from head to toe. Her teeth chattered, and her braids and skirt dripped water onto the hearth. He walked to the bedroom and returned with a towel and woman's dress, which he handed to her. Anna blanched when she realized the dress had belonged to Nalin.

"I'm sure you recall that she was quite a bit shorter than you are now. And thinner," he added unnecessarily. "But this fit her when she was pregnant." Carter took Paddy's hand and walked with him to the other room, giving Anna privacy.

She stripped out of her wet clothes, dried

her body and hair with the towel, and slipped into the dress. It was neither tight nor loose, but it was very short, ending right below her knees and revealing her bare calves and ankles. Her petticoat and bloomers would have given her legs coverage, but they were soaked and couldn't be worn. Her shoes and stockings were wet and muddy too, and she realized with dismay that she would have to present herself barefooted as well as bare-legged.

She looked at herself in the mirror and winced. She might as well be wearing a nightdress. Without underclothes, she could see the outline of her thighs through the dress. She had never felt so exposed and wondered whether she should ask Carter for a pair of Nalin's drawers. The very thought of asking him about his wife's unmentionables made her feel sick to her stomach. She couldn't bear to do it, and she realized she would have to resign herself to being immodest if she couldn't ask the question and also wished to remain dry.

What most concerned her was how Carter would react to seeing her in his late wife's dress. Anna took a deep breath and tried to comfort herself. It wasn't the worst thing to ever happen. She hadn't meant any harm. Carter would understand. Wouldn't he?

Mustering up as much courage as she could, she tapped on the bedroom door. "I'm finished changing." She turned away to avoid having to look at him and got to work making breakfast in the kitchen. The door opened, and Paddy scampered to Anna and latched onto a side of her skirt like he usually did.

Then Paddy said "mama" softly and Anna dropped a spoon. It clattered loudly on the floor. Anna felt ashamed and close to tears. She carefully bent at the knees to pick up the spoon and placed it soundlessly in the basin. The only noise for some time after that was the fire crackling and the rain beating on the roof. A wave of nausea rippled through her stomach and tightened around her throat. She knew that by wearing the dress she had broken some unspoken rule about how to act in front of a family who had lost their wife and mother. Why, oh why, hadn't she just stayed home?

Anna heard Carter move to the sofa. She was aware that he was watching her, but she avoided looking at him and poured her nervous energy into making breakfast, praying that she wouldn't need to run outside to be sick. She imagined that Carter thought many things, including how big and awkward she looked in his small wife's dress. She felt like a giant on display at a carnival. Every movement she made felt grotesque, and her cheeks burned with shame.

Eventually Carter spoke. "Anna, stop what you're doing and come sit by me. I want to speak with you."

Her heart skipped a beat and she almost burst into tears right then. As she trudged obediently to him, she realized she feared him more in that moment than she ever had before. He had never raised his voice at her, but Anna still had a horrible feeling she was about to be reprimanded. All of her emotions were raw and pooling at the surface. She felt ashamed, foolish, and exposed, and she knew that a single unkind word from him would make her cry. She sat on the opposite end of the sofa and pulled the skirt down to cover as much of her legs as possible. Her knees were trembling, and not from the cold.

"Are you feeling better now that you're dry?" he asked.

Anna didn't know how to respond. Nothing about the situation felt better to her. "I, I'm so sorry, Mr. Barnes," she stammered. "About wearing this dress. I didn't mean—"

"You needn't be sorry, Anna," he interrupted. "I'm afraid I don't know much about women's clothing. If you need something else, take it from the dresser."

She blushed, realizing that without a doubt he'd noticed she wore nothing under the dress. He knew she needed drawers.

"Thank you. I will look in the dresser. I'm sorry," she apologized again.

"Don't be," he relayed for the second time. His voice was gentle and inquisitive. "You've been trying very hard not to look at me for some time. Are you afraid of what I might think, seeing you in Nalin's dress?"

Anna felt distressed by his accurate assessment of her feelings. She gave him a pleading look that begged him not to make her explain how uncomfortable she felt. Much to her dismay, she felt a tickle in her nose and moisture in her eyes that indicated she was seconds from crying.

When he saw her face, Carter's gaze immediately turned apologetic. He glanced over at Paddy. Clearing his throat and taking a businesslike tone, he said, "How long have you been working here, Anna?"

She was reminded in that moment that although Carter was stern and sometimes impatient, one thing he wasn't was cruel. She would never forget his kindness in her most vulnerable state. Beyond grateful for the change in topic, she looked up to the ceiling for a few moments in recollection so she could answer his question accurately. "Five months, two weeks, and three days."

Paddy climbed into Carter's lap. Carter raised an eyebrow at her precise response, then said, "You're a hard worker and a good employee. I've half a mind to put you to work rounding cattle with my men, but they wouldn't like being shown what's what by a filly."

Anna felt overjoyed by his two sentences of praise. She could hardly believe what she'd just heard.

"Are you tired? Do you wish to be with your

friends and family more?" he asked.

"No, sir. I like working here. I'm saving the money too."

"That's smart. I thought you might be saving it. Except for all those sweets you buy, of course."

Paddy spoke up to request candy and ask about the rain clattering on the rooftop. Carter cut him off. "Paddy, hush when the grown-ups are talking. I'll answer your hundreds of questions later." Carter tickled him to soften the chiding.

It didn't go unnoticed by Anna that he'd acknowledged her as a grown-up, though she was only seventeen.

Seeming to read her mind, Carter asked, "How old are you, anyway?"

"I'll be eighteen next month."

"That's what I thought," he said, leaning back and pulling Paddy into a hug. "I'm sorry, honey, but it looks like you'll have to put up with me underfoot today. It's raining too hard for me to go out."

Anna stood and smoothed the dress down her front. "It's no bother, Mr. Barnes. I like it when you're here." She immediately regretted her candid remark and blushed.

She watched with wonder as she witnessed Carter's face ease into a smile for the first time since she could remember. His lips turned up more to one side than the other and revealed a dimple that transformed his stern face into a picture of boyish mischief.

"Call me Carter from now on," he said.

CHAPTER FIVE

Anna's eighteenth birthday fell on a Friday. Carter told her to take a paid day off, but she said she didn't want to. He decided not to insist but was annoyed by her refusal. Why couldn't the girl go have fun for a day? She was of marrying age. To find a worthy man, she'd have to spend some time in town meeting potential suitors, and she wasn't doing that while employed at his ranch. He'd recently become aware of how long and hard she worked for him, and he felt a bit guilty about it.

Carter had begun to notice the grown-up version of Anna. It took him by surprise to discover that the quiet girl was actually quite strong-willed. He liked the way she'd stood up to him when he accused her of spoiling Paddy. And when she broke the glass as payback for not speaking to her, he'd realized she was not someone he could ignore, nor did he want to from that point forward. It had required a great deal of self-control not to laugh in front of her the evening of the ruckus. He didn't want her to know how adorable he found her silly antic. By the look on her face, she thought she'd done something unforgivable, when really it was nothing but a naughty prank that begged for him to give her attention.

When he'd walked outside to dump the shards of glass, he'd continued a distance away from the cabin so he could release the laughter that had built up inside of him while he was sweeping. He had not felt such a thrill for a long time. For days he kept thinking about the wide-eyed expression she'd focused on him as he approached her. It made his palm itch to connect with her backside.

He felt an ache in his chest when he thought about the day she'd changed into Nalin's dress. The girl had sat beside him, so vulnerable and close to tears. Her face burned red-hot from embarrassment. As much self-control as it took to avoid laughing when she'd broken the glass, it took twice that to abstain from dragging the trembling girl onto his lap and hugging and kissing her to soothe away her obvious distress and shame. Rarely had he felt so compelled to console someone. An unexpected yearning to be comforted by her had struck him as well. Seeing his wife's dress worn in the present had brought emotions too painful to explore, but it had made him want the girl wearing the dress to put her arms around him.

He had recently noticed just how pretty and womanly Anna appeared, despite her childish braids and frilly dress. Her face was serene, if serious, and gave away her innocence and sincere regard for others. She was tall, just a few inches shorter than his six-foot frame, and full of voluptuous curves that she unknowingly revealed by moving around to do her work.

His favorite thing about Anna was her sensitivity, but it also frustrated him. The other day he watched, incredulous, as she worked for several minutes trying to cajole a mean-looking spider into climbing onto a stick. When it finally latched on after repeated failed attempts, Anna walked outside with it.

She came back in without the spider or stick, and Carter frowned at her. "What in the Sam Hill did you just do?"

"I put a spider outside so no one would get bit," she replied, as though that fully explained the last five minutes.

"Why didn't you just squash it?"

"I don't know. I didn't think of that."

Carter shook his head. "I don't know how you've managed to live on a farm without trying to save the life of every animal set for slaughter."

"I do try to save them," she said, sadness clouding her pretty face.

Those were the moments he felt frustrated. How could someone like that survive in this world, which he knew firsthand to be merciless?

* * *

Anna arrived on Friday morning.

Carter said, "Happy birthday, Miss Brown," and gave one of her braids a tug. He watched the color rise to her cheeks like it did whenever he paid her the slightest bit of attention, which he had been doing more of since the incident with the glass. She was light-skinned and blushed easily, and he noticed it every time she felt embarrassed. It awoke in him a tenderness that was almost painful.

He cleared his throat. "I'd like to take you to supper in town. You know, in celebration of your birthday. We could leave around four o'clock unless you have other plans. My foreman's wife Grace said she would stop by to watch Paddy."

"I don't have plans. That sounds nice," Anna said, smiling broadly. She looked delighted to spend time out with him, and it made him feel a few inches taller.

At four when Grace showed, Carter hooked up the buggy. They kissed Paddy good-bye and took off for town. When they arrived at the restaurant, Carter held Anna's hand to help her down, then positioned it so it was in the crook of his arm to escort her inside. Anna didn't object and even moved her hand around his arm to latch on better.

People looked up when they walked in. Most were familiar faces. A couple of Carter's ranch hands sat at a table on the other side of the restaurant drinking beer and whiskey. One yelled, "Hey, boss. Out to kick up a row tonight?"

Carter took off his Stetson. He placed it on the hat rack next to the door and walked to their table with Anna on his arm. "Joe, Sam—meet Anna. She's been minding my son and keeping house for me for some time now."

"Howdy," they both said.

"Hello," Anna responded in a shy voice, her hand still in the crook of his elbow. "It's nice to meet some other employees of Carter's."

Joe laughed rudely and slapped his palm on the table. He was drunk already. "You're his employee, you say? That's too dear."

Carter's temper flared, and he scowled. "Can't see as I get your meaning, Joe. That's what she is. Darn fine one too, which is more than I can say for half of you no-account saddle stumps."

"Whoa, whoa, hey," Joe said, raising his hands in surrender. "Just never thought of women's work that way is all. Didn't mean no offense."

"It's all right. I'm not offended," Anna piped up.

It rankled Carter that Anna smoothed over the disrespect and so quickly absolved the rowdy cowhand. She'd do well to clip his horns and make him mind his manners. His thoughts suddenly flashed to Nalin. She would've given the scamp a tongue-lashing that spun his head. Carter's only role would have been to admire the results of his spitfire wife's ire. Anna was different. More vulnerable, less fierce.

Carter wanted to move on to a better part of the evening, so he took their leave. "It's Anna's birthday and we're here to celebrate, so we'll be getting to it. Have a good night."

"See you tomorrow, boss. Nice to meet you, miss," Sam said.

Joe said nothing and downed a shot of whiskey.

Carter and Anna sat at a table with a red-checkered tablecloth. The waitress, who had been a friend to his wife, brought them a menu that listed two meals: fried chicken and turkey. A variety of dishes were available for the sides.

"How-do, Carter. Not seen you for a spell. How you holding up?"

Carter hated those kinds of well-intentioned and unavoidable questions. "Doing fine enough, thank you, Miss Black. Are you still attending those suffrage meetings?"

"Spotty, but yes. They've not had the same energy without Nalin. She was on the shoot every time. Smart as a whip and sharp as a bull's horn."

"Yes, that would be Nalin," Carter said.

Seeming to notice Anna for the first time, the waitress asked, "Who's the little girl you have here?"

"Sorry. Excuse my shoddy manners. This is Anna Brown, and she's not a little girl. In fact, she's eighteen today. She's between grass and hay, I'd say." Carter winked at Anna.

The waitress studied her. "Well, don't that beat all? Sorry, honey, I only saw the braids and not your pretty, grown-up face. And criminy! You're as tall as most men, so you're certainly not a nipper."

Anna smiled. "Nah, not been a nipper for a few moons now. It's nice to meet you."

"Same. Well, enough of my yammering. You can see there are two meals for the choosing tonight. Drink choices are the same as always, and we have raspberry cobbler and apple pie for dessert."

She left them alone to decide. They studied the menu for a minute. "What do you want to eat?" Carter asked.

Anna had stopped looking at the choices and was absentmindedly twirling a braid in between her fingers and staring into the distance. She focused her attention. "I'll have lemonade, turkey, green beans, red potatoes, corn-on-the-cob, and apple pie."

Carter coughed to muffle a laugh. "Is that all?"

She nodded seriously, not catching his amusement. He repeated her order to the waitress and ordered the other meal for himself.

While they ate, Anna remained quiet unless Carter asked her a question. He realized this was the way it had been for months, and he understood why. Throughout her time under his employ, whenever she spoke to him without first being spoken to, there was a good chance he would respond impatiently.

"Anna, I want you to feel like you can talk to me. I promise from now on I won't ignore you or behave impatiently like I have in the past. You've been a saint to put up with me."

"Thank you, Carter," she said, giving him the sweetest smile before returning her focus to the food on her plate.

He laughed, and she looked up at him with surprise. "What's so funny?"

"You, honey. I just told you to feel free to talk to me, and the first thing you did was get straight back to eating."

"I don't have anything to say."

"Fair enough."

She looked worried that she might have offended him. "I'm real tickled to be here, Carter. Thank you for taking me out for my birthday."

"It's my pleasure, believe me."

Soon he noticed that all the food on her dinner plate and dessert plate was gone. "You want me to order something else for you?" Carter asked, a smile playing on his lips.

"No, I'm full. Thanks."

She didn't understand that he was teasing her, so he pressed it further. "I'm thinking twice about giving you eating privileges at my house. Or maybe I should deduct a quarter from your pay now that I know how much you can eat."

Anna blushed but responded to his tease with a retort he didn't expect. "That's fine. Pretend you gave me a quarter raise and deduct that."

Carter laughed, very pleased with her response. He paid the bill and they walked to the buggy. On the way to Anna's house, Carter talked about the hot weather, his renewed plan for building a chicken coop, and the fact that the restaurant's vegetables had been overcooked. He said he liked the way she cooked vegetables better, then he asked her what type of chickens he should buy for his coop.

Anna listened mostly, still only speaking when he asked her a question.

It was dusk, and the path to her family's farm was empty. Carter pulled the horse to a halt halfway there and lifted the brake. Anna eyed him quizzically, and he answered her wordless question right away.

"All right, young lady, you're going to turn yourself over my lap. You've had a spanking coming for some time, and I intend to give it to you right now, right smart."

Anna gave him the wide-eyed expression he had anticipated.

"Lickety-split, or it'll be worse for you." Taking her arm, he guided the surprised yet compliant girl over his legs. The curve of her shapely bottom upturned on his lap was such a pretty site that he waited no longer than a second before he gave it a solid spank.

Anna gasped. "Carter, I don't understand."

"What don't you understand, darlin'?"

"I don't understand why you're spanking me!"

"Oh, that." He grinned and spanked her some more, the swats no harder than firm pats over her dress and petticoat. "Did you really think I'd let you get away with smashing that glass?"

She didn't respond, and he filled the silence with spanking.

"Hmm?" he prodded.

"I didn't do that on purpose," she said finally.

He stopped and exclaimed, "Balderdash and poppycock!" before continuing the spanking.

Much to his pleasure, Anna giggled. He planted a couple more mild swats. He didn't want to leave a sting. He only wanted her to know that he noticed her and would be giving her the attention she craved from then on.

"And another thing, I'm not pleased that you insisted on working today. It's your birthday, and I wanted you to go have fun."

"I did have fun, Carter. With you."

"Is that so? Are you having fun with me now?" He paused to hear her answer.

She only giggled her response.

He laughed and continued the smacks. "Lands sakes! You like being over my lap for a licking, don't you?"

"I most certainly do not!"

"You most certainly do. And that's twice now you've told a fib. Not the best idea while in this position. But this is a nice spanking and you're allowed. You'd be wise to avoid earning yourself a punishment licking. I'm not so agreeable during those."

Anna wriggled adorably in his lap. "You would punish me in this manner? Is that a bluff, or do you mean it for real?"

"You'd better believe I mean it. I would tan your hide right proper if you did something to deserve it. So far as I can tell, though, you're practically an angel from heaven."

He spanked her mildly a few times, then said, "Five more good ones, and after that I'll take you home. Are you ready?"

Anna squirmed again in his lap. "What if I say no?"

Carter grinned. "The same thing, but harder smacks."

To demonstrate, he gave her five quick, sharp swats that resembled those of a serious spanking, and she squealed and kicked up a foot. He lifted her to her spot next to him and released the brake. She turned her head away from him, embarrassed, but not before he caught the smile on her face.

He chuckled and said, "Giddy up." He slapped the reins on the horse and took the brand spankin' new woman the rest of the way home.

CHAPTER SIX

Carter built the chicken coop near the barn. He worked on it between herding cows, fixing fences, and training his two new colts, so it took him a few weeks to complete. Whenever he worked on it, Anna and Paddy visited him. Anna gave advice on the best way to structure the coop. She recommended using pine wood for the nests and motioned with her hands to suggest the size he should make them. Carter took every word of her advice.

It was on a hot day in September, while he sawed the wood for the nests, that he realized he was no longer in the stupor that had plagued him for so long. Though he still felt pangs of sadness at the loss of his wife, the pangs didn't last all day and all night like they had before. He felt other things besides pain and anger. He was able to laugh. Food tasted good to him again. He noticed that his son was growing and getting smarter by the day. And of course, he noticed Anna.

He knew that Anna's presence had helped him navigate through the devastating loss. It wasn't that Anna replaced Nalin. She was practically her opposite, both in appearance and personality. Nalin had been dark skinned; Anna was fair. Nalin had barely reached his chest in height; Anna was only a few inches shorter than he. As for personality, Nalin had been quick-witted and sarcastic. She was caring in her own way, but her tough exterior and sharp tongue veiled her concern for others. As tough as she was, she was also giddy and full of laughter—brighter and happier than anyone Carter had met, right up until her very last days. Fevered, weak, and minutes from death, she'd laughed when Carter sat next to her on the bed, held her hand, and told her Paddy had climbed from the floor, to a chair, to the counter and reached the highest shelf in the cabinet to retrieve the sweets she'd hidden. Her laughter was genuine but quickly turned into hacking coughs before she collapsed into sleep, never to wake again.

Anna, on the other hand, was quiet and serious and didn't laugh often. She was as demure as Nalin was combative. Carter appreciated her quiet presence during the sad months following his wife's death. He had not felt like talking or listening, and without Anna realizing it, she'd given him the space he needed to move past the worst of his grief.

As much as he felt comforted by having

Anna there at his house, he also felt uneasy. She was young and pretty, and by devoting all her waking hours to him and his son, she was foregoing the more pleasurable parts of life. Carter tried to ignore the discomfort he felt when he thought about her being courted by a man who surely wouldn't be worthy—that is, if she ever left his place long enough to find herself a suitor.

He smiled to himself, remembering how much food she ordered on her birthday and the way the color rose to her cheeks when he teased her about it. Her giggles over his lap had charmed him, and he found himself thinking about her the better part of his days.

Anna interrupted his thoughts. "Would you like a drink?" she asked, holding out a glass of cold lemonade.

Paddy stood next to her, pointedly not holding her hand. He was four years old now and had announced that he was too big to hold anyone's hand, although he still made his way to their laps often enough.

"Thanks," Carter said. He put down the saw and held the glass in his gloved hand. He finished all of the lemonade in three gulps. "That was delicious."

Anna reached over and took the empty glass from him.

Carter noticed her studying him. He had rolled up his sleeves, so his arms were bare from the elbow down and slick with sweat produced by exertion and the relentless Texas heat. He wondered what she thought when she looked at him. He hoped her thoughts were favorable.

Turning to Paddy, he asked, "Will you help me with some of this work, little man?"

Paddy nodded his head and grinned. He never turned down an opportunity to help his pa.

"Take these scraps of wood and set them by the firewood in the shed," he said.

The chore would have taken Carter one trip but would require a good twenty minutes for Paddy to complete. Carter knew this, of course, but he also knew it was important for his son to feel useful and keep busy. He caught Anna smiling at him knowingly, and he smiled back. She looked sunburned and happy, and she wore a new dress. It was a woman's dress, calico and lace, and it was green, matching her eyes. It made her look five years older.

"I like your new duds," Carter said.

"Thank you. I sewed this dress at home on Sundays."

"Is there anything you can't do?"

Anna blushed. Carter found her more exquisite with every passing day.

❈ ❈ ❈

Since Carter never told Anna what she could or couldn't do, and because she was less fearful of him after witnessing him slowly returning to his former self, she began to take some liberties at his ranch. One such liberty was visiting the three-year-old grey stallion named Tuck that Carter kept in the first stall of the barn. Whenever Paddy took a nap, she wandered out to feed the horses carrots or sugar cubes. She loved Bella, the docile mare that had been around since she was a child, but Tuck excited her. Carter hadn't trained the stallion to be ridden. Instead, the horse's primary purpose was as a stud to his broodmares.

Other than learning from Carter how to behave properly on the lead, Tuck was as wild as they came. Anna liked that he was full of vibrancy and personality. Tuck quickly learned that when Anna showed up, he would get treats, so he nickered every time he saw her. He would continue to make noises at her until she gave him her full attention, stamping his front foot impatiently. After a week of visiting him, she felt bold enough to enter Tuck's stall instead of feeding him from the outside. She stepped in and stroked his neck and back. When he responded by nuzzling her, she continued the habit of entering his stall every day.

Anna remembered spending time in the same barn as a child. Her parents had gone on a business trip when she was around eight years old, and the Barnes were looking after her and her sisters. Tuck wasn't around back then, but Carter had owned several mares that she'd liked to pet, including Bella.

One day, he'd shown up at the barn suddenly and pulled her down from Bella's back. "Anna, do me a favor and tell someone next time you're going somewhere. Don't just leave every time you get a bee in your bonnet."

She grinned up at him. "I did tell someone I was leaving. I told Spot."

Carter rolled his eyes. "You know what I mean. Tell someone with only two legs and less fur."

She giggled with delight at his words, and he gave her a small smile in return.

When Anna had entered the cabin holding Carter's hand, Nalin looked up. Relief flooded her face upon seeing Anna but was quickly replaced with annoyance. She put her hands on her hips. "Where were you? I couldn't find you anywhere."

"I was out in the barn with Bella. I'm sorry, Mrs. Barnes. I didn't mean to be unfindable. I was just saying howdy to the horses."

Nalin turned her frown to Carter. "I hope you explained that she's to tell one of us next time she goes off somewhere."

"I do believe I did, didn't I, Anna?"

She nodded. "Yes."

Carter released her hand and strode to his armchair, where he sat down and picked up his newspaper.

Nalin looked at Anna. "How do you feel about helping me bake some bread?"

"I'd like that."

"Good. It should keep you out of trouble for the rest of today at least. I'm trying a new recipe. It's honey bread. We can learn how to make it together, and you can give me some tips if you think of any."

Anna and Nalin worked on mixing the ingredients and kneading the bread. Anna's only advice was to add more honey.

Nalin talked to her about the latest dime novel she'd purchased. She said she liked to read about other people's adventures. "I don't much care for getting into dangerous scrapes myself, but I like reading about them."

Anna pushed her floured hands into the dough. "I like danger and adventure, but I hate reading."

Nalin laughed. "I don't know too many people who like danger. Make sure you don't do anything silly. I don't want you to get hurt."

"I'll be careful, Mrs. Barnes."

The honey bread turned out to be delicious, and Carter complimented them. "If you two made bread like that every day, I'd never leave the cabin."

Nalin snorted. "That would be unbearable. I'll be sure not to make it too often."

The next second, Carter was charging her. She threw flour in his face and ran. He chased her into a corner and she shrieked with laughter as he grabbed her.

❋ ❋ ❋

Anna smiled at the memory. Nalin had a quick wit and a fast laugh. She and Carter had been good together. Out of nowhere, Anna felt tears welling up in her eyes. Although her grief was nothing like Carter's, she missed Nalin too. Nalin was a smart woman who spoke her mind just like a man. Anna had viewed her as an older sister, and she'd confided in Nalin throughout the years without the fear of judgment. Anna decided she'd tell Carter just that. She hadn't expressed any thoughts about Nalin since her death out of fear that it wasn't her place, but she felt that by now she and Carter might be in a place to discuss it.

Anna thought of Nalin on her way to the barn one early afternoon to visit Tuck. She thought of her promise to Nalin that she would be careful and not do anything silly. She felt a bit guilty then, entering the stall of the dangerous stallion, but the memory of Nalin's admonishment wasn't enough to stop her.

She saw Tuck's ears pop up and heard his familiar nicker. What she didn't see or hear was Carter on the other side of the barn grooming one of his mares. Anna headed straight for Tuck's stall. She unlatched and swung the door open so she could join him. She patted him on the neck and fed him three carrots, breaking each one in two so she could feed him from her hand six times. She liked the feeling of his soft nose and whiskers tickling her palm when he picked the carrot up with his lips.

She heard a noise and turned with a start to find Carter at the stall's opening. His right hand rested on the corner of the swinging door. His left hand held a quirt. Her surprise turned to apprehension. She wondered if Carter would be angry at her for not asking permission first before entering Tuck's stall. Carter moved into the stall and rubbed Tuck's neck. "That's good, Tuck," he said in a deep, soothing voice. "Back up now." Carter tapped the top of his shoulder with the whip. Tuck retreated away from the door, which put Anna better in his reach. He took a firm hold of her arm and pulled her out of the stall. He closed the door and dragged her to a two-person bench against the wall of the barn, where he set her down in the middle of it. He towered above her.

"What were you doing? Where's Paddy? How long have you been visiting Tuck?" he asked. His words tumbled out quickly. He looked furious.

Anna hated to see him angry. Before, she would have only felt fear, but now she felt fear and concern that he would have a bad opinion of her. She looked down at her hands. "Paddy's taking a nap. I've been visiting Tuck for a few weeks now maybe."

He sucked in a breath and raised his voice. "That stallion is dangerous. All studs are, but him especially because he wasn't socialized properly before I got him."

Anna looked up and said to him in a pleading voice, "I've been really careful. I know stallions are dangerous, Carter."

"I don't think you do know. Prior to seeing you, I was planning to walk my mare straight past Tuck's stall on the way out the barn. Do you know what might have happened if I had?" Carter's scowl deepened. "Tuck's stall door was wide open. You would have been the only thing standing between him and a mare in heat, and he would have trampled you if it meant he could get to her a minute faster."

Anna's eyes filled with tears as he spoke. She felt misunderstood and wanted him to know she wasn't ignorant. She knew the danger.

"Yes, sir. I know. I don't know how to explain it, but I like being around danger sometimes. It makes me feel excited."

Carter's expression softened, but only slightly. "I know that about you, Anna. I've known that since a decade ago when I carried you down from that tree out front. And I do understand the feeling." He cleared his throat. "The thing is, Anna, while I do understand, I can't allow it. You're not to visit Tuck again without me here. Are we in agreement?"

Anna's heart sank. She looked past Carter at Tuck, feeling like she had just lost a friend.

"Can I still give him carrots from outside the stall when you're not around?"

"No."

She bit her lip and looked down, determined not to cry. "All right," she said, her voice betraying her disappointment.

"Look at me."

Anna lifted her sorrowful eyes up to his.

Carter grunted with frustration. He moved to Tuck's stall to double-check that the door was latched. He turned back to Anna who was still eyeing him. "Blast! I don't like seeing that look on your face. It makes me feel powerfully mean."

His words made her forget her own disappointment for a moment, and she felt compelled to comfort him. "It's all right, Carter. I understand why you won't let me. Don't feel bad."

Carter shook his head and stared at her with disbelief. "You're trying to make *me* feel better? You really are an angel, aren't you, Anna?

Anna felt her disappointment fade a bit. Her face took on a small smile. She wondered what Carter would say if she told him another secret. "I'm not an angel," she informed him.

"No?"

"I found the whiskey in your cellar."

The muscles in Carter's face relaxed. "Is that right?"

"Yes. And I drank some of it."

His eyes twinkled. He ambled toward her. "Anything else you'd like to confess?"

"No, sir."

Carter face broke into his boyish smile, displaying his dimple dent. "Lucky for you I'm not one of those men who thinks it's unladylike for a woman to drink. In fact, that was Nalin's whiskey, truth be told."

Leaning down, he kissed Anna on the forehead, which took her breath away almost as much as his next words.

"Stand up, Anna, and turn around."

Her eyes widened. She stood slowly. He didn't look angry anymore, but he was still holding the quirt. "Are you going to whip me?" she asked, her voice pitiful and far less brave than she would have liked.

"Yes, honey. Only twice, and not to punish you. It's to communicate something very important, lest my leniency today gives you the wrong idea."

She turned to face the wall. A few seconds later she felt the moderate sting of two smacks on her heavily clad bottom. She winced, but the strokes didn't sting enough to make her cry out. Taking her arm, Carter guided her around to face him again.

"Think about that if you're tempted to visit Tuck again. This is your first time doing something truly dangerous since you started working for me, so I don't have it in me to be hard on you. However, I won't hesitate to apply that whip ten more times if you give me cause to fear for your safety again, and I'll make sure there's fewer layers of protection on your unfortunate bottom."

Anna could tell he meant it.

He hung the quirt next to a halter on the

stall and looked at her. "I hope you don't learn the hard way that it's almost as dangerous to disobey me as it is to visit that stallion."

Anna looked down at her hands. "No, sir, I won't learn it the hard way."

"Good girl."

CHAPTER SEVEN

It was a pleasant, warm morning, and Anna was late. That never happened, so Carter felt uneasy and decided to go look for her. He was exiting the bedroom after retrieving his riding gloves when the door swung open and Anna stumbled in. She didn't stop but headed straight into his surprised embrace. He held her briefly, enjoyed the feeling of her warm body against his, then took hold of her arms and held her out to look at her. Upon seeing her face, he took in a sharp breath. Her left eye was swollen and her nose was bleeding.

"What happened?" He cupped her chin and turned her face in both directions. Despite the initial shock of seeing her hurt, he relaxed. She wasn't seriously injured. "You're a bit banged up there, honey," he said, moving his hand to rest on his hip.

"I'm sorry I'm late," she said, breathing hard.

"It happened at the fork in the road."

The fork was about three-quarters of a mile from his place and therefore closer to her family's cabin than to his. He wondered why she didn't go home after getting injured instead of running all the way to his place. He would question her about that later.

Meanwhile, Carter looked around and found a clean rag. He plunged it into the basin, wrung it so it wouldn't drip, and walked to her side. He led her to the sofa, where they sat down and he blotted the blood from her face. He felt along her nose and jaw with his fingertips.

"Nothing's broken. Are you sore anywhere else?"

"No. He only slugged me in the face. It was because I didn't have any money." Her bottom lip protruded into a pout.

Carter's eyes froze on her. "What? I thought you fell. You mean to tell me someone hit you?"

"Yes."

He tightly controlled his anger so that he could ask her calmly, "Did you recognize him?"

"One of the older Ferry kids," she replied.

The Ferry family had ten children, give or take, all running wild. The parents were known for shady dealings in trade. The kids ranged in age from nineteen to eight, and most were bullies and troublemakers.

Anna sniffled. He reached over and pulled her to his chest. He wrapped his arms around her, which caused her to release the cries she was holding back. Carter became angrier with every tear she shed.

After some time, Carter took her arms near her shoulders and pried her away. "That's enough, Anna. You'll run out of tears for the next time you want to cry."

Anna hiccupped. "I'm sorry about your shirt," she said weakly, pointing to the large wet patch on his chest.

"You will be when you're washing it," he said with a wry smile, hoping to make her laugh.

It worked and she did laugh softly, still hiccupping. He stood and found a handkerchief so she could blow her nose. He handed it to her, crossed his arms in front of his chest, and looked down at the sniffling girl on his sofa. She looked a mess. Her face was red, wet, and puffy. Weeds protruded from her braids, and a side of her new dress was covered in dirt. Carter knew this meant the brute hit her hard enough to make her fall to the ground. Anger brewed stronger inside of him with every passing second.

"Are you all right?" he asked through gritted teeth.

Anna nodded and blew her nose carefully, looking pained.

Carter's hands closed into fists as he walked to the door. "This won't happen again."

"What are you going to do?"

He grabbed his Stetson. "I haven't decided yet." He shut the door shut behind him and left for town on his horse.

Hours later, when Carter returned to the cabin, he entered to find Anna patching a hole in a pair of his denims. She looked clean from a bath, and the swelling on her eye had gone down considerably. Paddy was in the bedroom napping.

Carter took his trousers from her. "Please rest, honey. Don't work today."

She put away her needle and patches of cloth and closed her sewing kit. She looked up at him. "What happened?" she asked.

"It was the oldest kid, John Ferry, who attacked you. He's lucky all I did was drag him to the marshal instead of giving him a taste of his own medicine. He's in jail for the night now. You needn't worry about him or anyone else from that family. I made it clear…" Carter didn't finish his sentence. He walked to his armchair and sat down.

"Made what clear?"

His voice was low. "I made it clear that the next person who hurt you would lose a lot more than his freedom for a day." He leaned back and closed his eyes. When he opened them, Anna was in the kitchen picking up the frying pan.

Carter reproached her. "Didn't I tell you to rest? Go lie down."

He noticed her shoulders become tense for a moment, but she responded with insistence in her voice. "I'm fine, Carter. I just want to make some supper."

"Absolutely not," he said. He was by her side in a flash taking the frying pan from her hand. "You can either rest here or I can take you home to rest there. Your choice."

Anna glared at him. She huffed and moved to a stool at the kitchen table instead of lying down, a variance to his order that he tolerated. Carter placed a pot of water over the fire. When it started to boil, he added beans. That and some leftover bread would have to do for supper. Turning, he leaned back against the counter and looked at Anna. The stubborn way she'd insisted on working and the brief flash of rebellion he'd seen in her eyes had riled him. Now sitting at the table, she wore such a forlorn expression that he considered taking her into his arms again, but he decided instead to give her a scolding. "What should I do with you, Anna Brown?"

The expression on her face changed from forlorn to confused. "What do you mean?"

"I mean that you don't seem to know what's best for you. You come to my place in the pouring rain and try to walk home when it's dark. You've put yourself in dangerous situations multiple times with my stallion." Carter's scowl deepened and he crossed his arms. "Today you ran all the way here instead of going home after getting hurt, and just now you tried to work when you should be resting. I even told you to rest, but you disobeyed me." His voice lowered. "People don't usually disobey me. At least not without paying for it."

Anna's confused expression evolved into apprehension as he spoke. She looked down and mumbled something he couldn't hear.

"Pardon?"

"Never mind," she said in the direction of the table, a trace of defiance in her voice.

Carter's voice took a warning tone. "I'm tempted to teach you a lesson right now about your reckless behavior and what may come of disobeying me."

Anna looked up. "What kind of lesson?"

"I think you know what kind." Carter opened a drawer and picked up a wooden spoon. He slapped it against the palm of his hand several times and fixed a hard look on her.

Anna stood and glowered at him. "Are you saying you're going to spank me with that?"

"I have half a mind to. Don't you think you deserve it?"

"No! I'm not a child, Carter. You seem to have forgotten that." She straightened her back and moved toward the front door. "I don't have to listen to this," she threw at him over her shoulder.

"Actually," he said, walking toward her, "you do have to listen. Don't forget who's in charge here. I'm your boss, and when I tell you not to do something, it's more than a suggestion."

Anna looked at him with her mouth slightly open and her eyes flashing between anger and worry. She settled on anger and held her head higher. "Do you threaten to spank all your employees, Carter?"

He almost smiled. That was the exact moment he realized he loved her. He loved the way she asked that question haughtily but with trepidation in her voice. He loved that she had run to him for help when she'd been hurt. He loved the way she cared about every person and creature around her with so much devotion that he'd been compelled to start caring again too.

"No, I don't threaten to spank all my employees. Only a certain young lady I happen to care about. Now stop fuming and go sit down. Smoke's going to come out of your ears in a minute."

Anna let out an affronted sigh. She sat back down and kicked a leg of the table.

"Oh, honey...," he said slowly. It hurt him not to turn her over his knee for that. "I promise you don't want to test me right now. Certainly don't be kicking the furniture if you care to sit for the rest of the evening." Carter put the wooden spoon back in the drawer. He checked the beans and began to slice the bread.

A few minutes passed before Anna spoke in a small voice. "Carter?"

"Yes, Anna?" His back was turned to her.

"You're not really going to punish me, are you? I didn't mean to do anything wrong." Her voice was meek.

There she is, Carter thought, smiling to himself. His angelic Anna was back. *His Anna.* It was the first time he allowed himself think of her possessively.

CHAPTER EIGHT

Anna's heart pounded. She had never raised her voice to Carter, and she was unsettled by how angry she'd gotten when he came close to giving her a real punishment. The truth was that in addition to feeling angry, she also felt exhilarated. The detached, grieving side of Carter had been ebbing for some time, but today it had disappeared completely and was replaced by the passionate, fearsome cowboy slicing bread in front of her.

For so long she had wished for him to pay attention to her and care about what she did. Today she'd gotten more attention than she'd bargained for. Carter had comforted her in his arms when she was hurt. He shook with anger when he found out she'd been attacked. He ordered her to obey him, scolded her, and threatened her with punishment. To Anna, all of his words and actions were exciting because they showed her that he cared for her like she cared for him, but they were also frightening to experience. In the not-too-distant past, he had barely looked up from his pipe and paper when she walked in the room. It was impossible for her to manage appropriately all of the feelings she was having in response to this change between them, so she'd reacted with anger, the strongest emotion in her reach.

She closed her eyes and let out a deep sigh. She wanted to please Carter, and she worried that he was disappointed in her and might still spank her. He had put that awful spoon away, but maybe he intended to use something else to punish her with. She was coming close to crying again, overwhelmed with conflicting emotions, when she felt his hand on hers. His touch settled her thoughts. Every touch of his was imprinted on her memory. A brush on the shoulder, his hand holding hers when she exited the buggy, his arms wrapping around her earlier that day, and, most breathtaking of all, the kiss he'd given to her forehead.

Carter's voice was gentle. "Anna, it was a bit hard of me to give you a dressing-down after what you've been through today. You're a very good girl, and your offenses are minor except for the stallion visits, which we've already settled. I'm not going to spank you."

Anna looked at his large hand on top of hers. Her thoughts spun in strange new directions. Part of her felt relieved that he wasn't going to punish her. The other part felt out of sorts, like maybe the fact that he was letting her off the hook meant he didn't care after all. She imagined what it would be like to lie helpless across his lap and feel his hard hand striking her bottom over and over, making her pay for her recklessness and disobedience. She wanted to be in that position, she realized. It would be thrilling, stimulating... *dangerous*. She wanted to belong to him and for him to punish her because she was his to punish.

She looked up. His eyes were so kind that she felt a rush of courage. "I want you to punish me," she said, hardly believing she was saying it out loud.

Her words hung unacknowledged in the air for far too long. She was afraid he would laugh, but he didn't. He lifted an eyebrow and said, "Why's that, Anna?"

"I don't know, really. I suppose I want to feel..." Anna couldn't think of how to express herself.

Another moment of silence hovered between them. "Feel that I care about you?" Carter finished for her.

"Yes," Anna said, relieved that he understood and she didn't have to explain.

He smiled and squeezed her hand before letting it go. "I care about you more than you know. A spanking can be arranged if you need proof of that, but not today when you're banged up. If you still think you need some of my painful attention on Friday, I'll spank you then."

Anna nodded her understanding. He gave her braid a tug before retrieving Paddy from the room and serving the measly supper.

* * *

The next morning, Anna's father showed up at the cabin with Anna. Carter poured coffee for him and milk for Anna. The only sign leftover from Anna's attack was slight bruising around her eye. The swelling was gone.

"Can't thank you enough for seeing to that bully yesterday," Paul said. "Anna told me what happened."

Carter had planned to visit Anna's parents that evening to discuss a few matters, but now that Paul was at his house, he decided to use the opportunity to let him in on his thoughts.

"Paul, I'm glad you came out with Anna today. There's a couple things I'd like to ask you about. Will you come see my new chicken coop?"

"Of course."

Leaving Anna and Paddy behind, the men walked to the coop Carter had built.

"You've done a bang-up job here," Paul said, looking it over with admiration. "What did you want to ask about it?"

"Thanks, Paul. Not sure whether she told you, but Anna helped me build it. She's actually what I wanted to talk to you about, not the coop."

"Oh?" Paul asked. "What about her?"

"I can't stomach the thought of her getting hurt again walking to my cabin. I did some thinking, and I'm of the opinion that she should ride here and back. I want to give her one of my horses. Would that be agreeable to you?"

"That's real generous of you, cowboy," Paul said. "It would put my mind at ease for sure."

Carter took a deep breath. He was nervous about asking the next question, despite their longstanding friendship. Paul was his elder by ten years and Carter had a respect for him that resembled that for an older brother. He knew the question he was about to ask would change their friendship forever.

He asked quickly before he lost his nerve. "Would you consent to me marrying Anna in the future?"

The question took Paul by surprise. He cocked his head. "Did I hear you right?"

Carter rested his hand on the gate of the coop and looked at the hills in the distance. "Yes. I want to marry her. I love her and I would bet my entire ranch that she's sweet on me too. But I don't want to ask for her hand just yet. I'd hate for her to consent before I courted her properly."

Paul smiled at him. "I have no objections, if you love her like you say. You're a good man, and Anna has turned into a fine woman."

"She certainly has."

Paul frowned at him. "What's this about

wanting to court her though? You see her every day."

"That's the problem. She works for me, and I don't want her working for me when I ask for her hand. I want to work for her. I want to give her gifts and take her for Sunday rides in the buggy."

Paul scoffed. "If she already loves you, I hardly see the point of that."

"Still," Carter said, "As soon as I can stand to let her go for a bit and find someone else to watch Paddy, I want to go about wooing her before getting hitched."

Paul put a hand on his shoulder. "Can't say as I understand your reasoning, but it's your right to take your time."

"Promise me you won't let her know my intentions just yet."

Paul shook his head. "It ain't for me to say. You have my word."

CHAPTER NINE

It was four days until Friday, the day of the spanking, and Anna felt butterflies in her stomach all four days. When Carter led her to the barn after her father left, she wondered if he'd decided not to wait and was going to spank her then. She was in for a different kind of surprise. He held her hand and took her to a stall in the back, one she knew well and visited often.

"Do you remember Bella?" he asked. "This is the horse I found you mounted on when you were a lass."

"I do remember. And I've been visiting her more ever since you forbade me from visiting Tuck." She frowned at him.

Carter raised an eyebrow. "You're still bellyaching about that?"

She shrugged. "I feel I have the right to complain."

"You don't. It's disrespectful."

Carter's chiding compelled her to be even

more disrespectful. "Hang it all. Fine, you won't hear another word about it from me."

Carter folded his arms. "A 'yes, sir' would have been a more acceptable response."

"Oh? I'm sorry about that," Anna said sarcastically, then grinned up at him.

Carter stared at her for a long time with an unreadable expression. She couldn't tell whether he was amused or annoyed.

Anna's grin turned into a soft smile and she looked down, indicating her surrender. She didn't know why she felt like giving him a hard time, except that it was kind of fun and a little dangerous.

"Anyway..." Carter said, giving her a sidelong glance before he opened the stall door. Bella butted him in his chest with her head, sending him a step back. He took her head in his hands and rubbed the white star between her eyes.

"She's not supposed to push like that. It's rude and would earn any other horse a little smack, but I allow it from her because we're old friends and she's tolerated plenty of mistakes from me over the years. She's the first horse I ever trained. I was just a lad of fifteen or sixteen when she was born."

Anna held the back of her hand up to Bella's nose. Bella sniffed and then turned and pushed into Carter again affectionately. This time Carter grunted in annoyance and gave her head a shove back. "Quit it," he said.

"It's hard for me to imagine you at age sixteen. What were you like?" Anna asked. She ran her hand down Bella's neck to her shoulder.

"I don't know. Younger. More handsome."

"That's impossible," Anna said, looking up at him with a shy smile.

"You think I'm handsome, do you?"

"Of course. Don't you think I'm pretty?"

Carter snorted. "If I tell you you're pretty, it's not going to be because you asked me."

"Fine. You don't have to say it. I already know you think I am," she informed him.

Carter stared at her again before clearing his throat. "We were talking about Bella, I believe. Do you still like her?"

"I love her. She's beautiful," Anna said.

"I'm glad you think so because I want to give her to you. She's yours."

"Really?" Anna squealed with delight but sobered quickly. "Won't you miss her though?"

Carter gave her one of his mildly frustrated looks. "No, I will not miss her. I'll see her practically every day. I want you to ride her back and forth from my place to yours. Your pa and I don't think you should walk anymore."

"I always wanted a horse," she said, her eyes shining. "Thank you, Carter."

"You're welcome." He winked at her.

Anna touched his arm. "Carter, I've been meaning to tell you something ever since that day you found me with Tuck. I hope it won't raise your bristles what I have to say. Perhaps I shouldn't say it, but I have a hankering to right now."

"Go on."

"I have fond memories of Mrs. Barnes. Of Nalin. I want you to know she was like an older sister to me. She told me not to be silly and put myself in danger, and I thought of her words and felt guilty when I visited Tuck that day you found me." Anna bit her lip and looked down for a moment, telling herself not to cry before she continued. Looking back up, she said, "I'm not sure if you remember, but the first time she baked honey bread, it was with me. I've never forgotten that recipe. I loved her, but not just because she taught me how to bake bread. I loved her because she was modern and smart and made me laugh. I just want you to know that I miss her too sometimes. I don't know anyone alive who's like her."

Carter's dark eyes never wavered from hers while she spoke, and she watched with dismay as they filled with tears.

"I'm sorry!" she cried. "Forgive me. I shouldn't have said anything."

Carter moved forward and hugged her to him tightly. "You have nothing to be sorry about, Anna. You are so kind, honey. What you said means a great deal to me, and I'm grateful. I loved Nalin for many reasons, including those you mentioned. You're right, there's no one else like her in the world. She was altogether special and that you noticed too makes me feel I'm not alone. Honey, you're so kind to tell me," he repeated, running a hand over her head.

Anna felt a tear streaking her face. "You're not alone, Carter. I don't ever want you to feel lonely."

"Thank you, sweetheart. I appreciate it, all right?" He released her from his grip and tipped her chin up to meet his eyes. "You can always trust me to accept and listen to what's on your mind about sensitive matters, including Nalin. Everything you say to me will be welcome to my ears. Will you trust that I mean that?"

"Yes, sir."

"Good girl."

Bella let out a low bellow and they focused their attention back to her.

"Tell me something, Anna. In giving you a horse, I'm assuming you know how to ride, but is that true?" He wiped a tear discreetly from his cheek.

She considered his question, wishing to answer honestly. She had ridden plenty of times but had never taken proper instruction from a cowboy.

"I know how to stay on," she said.

Carter smiled. "That's a start. Let's have a little lesson, shall we?"

Anna nodded but then looked down at her dress. "I don't know if I can ride in this," she said.

Carter examined her skirt. "You're right.

That doesn't look too comfortable for riding. Next time I'm in town, I'll buy you a suit for riding."

"You don't have to do that. I can make one," she said. "You already gave me a horse, after all!"

"I want to get it for you, and anything else you might want or need. But in the meantime, let's see if we can't still have a short lesson. I'll give you a leg up. See if your dress will let you straddle her."

Carter put a hand under her bent leg and lifted while Anna swung her other leg around Bella's back. Her skirt and petticoat were wide and loose enough that she only had to hike them up a bit, revealing her legs up to her knees the same way she had when she'd worn Nalin's dress. She wasn't embarrassed this time.

"It looks like that will work. Feel comfortable enough for a quick ride?" Carter asked. Anna nodded and he helped her down. "Let's tack her up and head for the corral."

Carter showed Anna the gear—blanket, pad, saddle, cinch, bridle, and halter. "This all comes with Bella," he said. "Over by the hitching post are the brushes and hoof picks. Give her a quick brush and clean her hooves every time you ride."

Carter strapped the halter on Bella and led her to the post, where he tethered her loosely. He picked up a hoof pick from the tack box and turned to address Anna. "Now before we start, I want to say a couple things in warning. I know you have a soft spot for animals. And spiders," he added, rolling his eyes.

Anna burst out laughing, and Carter lifted an eyebrow. "I don't think I've ever heard you laugh so hard."

She was still laughing when she said, "I can't believe you remembered that. And I'm just so happy right now."

"I'll let you finish before I continue." He gave her a look of mock impatience and she dissolved into a new wave of giggles.

When she collected herself, Carter said, "It's good to have compassion for animals, but you always need to protect yourself. If your horse decides to buck or take off in a gallop without your permission, you do whatever it takes to stop her. That's what the bit is for. If she butts into you like she did to me, give the lead rope a hard jerk. I'm a tough old whacker, but her doing that to you could send you to the ground. Make sense?"

"Yes, sir," she said.

"Now I'm not too worried about Bella putting you in harm's way. She doesn't spook easily, but a horse is a horse. It's best to be prepared and always have a healthy respect for a horse's strength."

He slid his hand down the inside of Bella's left front leg, and she lifted her foot off the ground. "As you can see, she'll lift her hoof for you at the slightest touch." He cleaned the debris, then handed the pick to Anna.

"Go ahead and give it a go."

Anna had cleaned hooves many times, but

she knew Carter would want to make sure she knew how to do it properly and she was glad to demonstrate and make him proud. She moved to Bella's back left hoof and imitated Carter, sliding her hand down the inside of Bella's leg. Bella lifted and Anna cleaned out her hoof, correctly pushing the pick down the two lines of the frog to clear the dirt and pebbles.

"Very good," he said, and Anna's heart swelled at his praise.

Carter brushed Bella while Anna cleaned out the other two hooves. "I'm going to leave you two alone for now and go check on Paddy. I want you to tack her up, then I'll check to make sure everything looks right before you start riding. Sound good?"

"Sounds great," Anna said. She could hardly believe she had a horse now. The only other animal she could call her own was a rooster her father agreed not to slaughter when Anna became unusually attached. Now that she owned a beautiful horse, Anna felt ready to burst with happiness.

Bella stood patiently while Anna worked on positioning the blanket, pad, and saddle. She adjusted and readjusted them a few times. Unsatisfied, she took everything off and started over. Finally, she moved to buckling the straps. Bella didn't like the cinch but accepted the tightening with a toss of her head. When Anna pulled the bridle over Bella's head, Bella opened her mouth to accept the bit before Anna even pressed it to her lips.

"Such a sweet girl," she murmured. "I wish I had a carrot for you."

Carter cleared his throat and Anna looked up to find him leaning against a stall with his arms crossed and a smile on his face. She wondered how long he'd been watching her. "I knew you'd be good with her. Let's see how you did with the saddle, huh? It looks good from here."

Anna fastened the buckles of the bridle while Carter inspected the saddle. He pulled at the cinch. "The cinch is too loose. That's important to get right, since it's dangerous to ride if the saddle isn't on tight."

Carter held the reins while Anna made the belly band a notch tighter. She felt how tight it was, then Carter tested it. "That's good. Check it one more time right before you mount. Horses sometimes puff up with air while being saddled to make the cinch feel tight to us. That way it'll be looser when they exhale. They're smart like that."

Carter looked at the bridle and found nothing wrong. He handed her the reins. "The mounting block is out to the left of the barn."

Anna took the reins and walked Bella to the block. Carter followed behind them. Anna stepped on the block, gathered the reins in her left hand, and slid a foot into the stirrup.

"Are you forgetting anything?"

Anna removed her foot from the stirrup and blinked at him. "Oh," she exclaimed. She checked the cinch again. "It feels just as tight to me." She gave him a questioning look to see if she should continue.

Carter walked over and took the reins from her hands. "Get off the block," he said.

"Why?"

"You'll find out."

Anna obeyed and stepped down. She stood close to Carter and looked up at him. He was so close she could smell him, and she drew a deep breath. He smelled like leather and cherry tobacco and soap. Stubble darkened his face, like usual. He didn't like to shave, but he wouldn't commit to a beard either.

Carter folded the reins a couple times in his hands while looking down at her. "I don't want you to forget to check the cinch again," he said. "You could get seriously hurt if you ride when it's too loose."

"I won't," Anna said, feeling chastened. She looked into his eyes, which were soft and kind without a trace of sternness.

"I'm going to make sure you don't forget. In the future, I want you to remember what's about to happen. Think about it before you mount and let it be a reminder for you to check the cinch."

"What's going to happen?" Anna asked, feeling her stomach clench into knots. She felt confused because his scolding words weren't matching his tone of voice.

With his free hand, he reached around to the

nape of her neck and pulled her head toward him.

"This," he said, and tilted his head down. He paused before he touched his lips to hers, giving her a chance to break free if she desired. When she didn't move, he kissed her and lingered on her lips. Anna closed her eyes. No man had kissed her on the lips before, and she didn't know what she was supposed to do. All she knew was that she didn't want it to end. When she felt his lips beginning to retreat, she kissed him back, holding his bottom lip between hers. She sucked at him with hunger and determination to make the kiss continue. Carter moved back in, capturing her needy lips in his and massaging them open. She felt his tongue flick hers. She was timid at first. She kept her tongue in place while his rubbed around hers. In time, she moved her tongue with his. The growing sensation in its nerves gave her a thrill she had never known before. She needed more. She thrust greedily into his mouth, feeling every part of the new territory with a sense of urgency. They continued to explore each other, alternating between forceful and gentle until together they retreated and ended where they started, with lips held together in a final moment of tenderness. They unlocked and Anna simmered in rapt silence.

When she opened her eyes, Carter was looking at her with astonishment. He had taken a step back. He moved his hand to his forehead and lifted his hat a little off his head. Then he unbuttoned the top few buttons of his shirt and ran a hand over his face. He tried to say something but then cleared his throat instead. He was speechless, she realized. She felt a power that she had never felt before—power over a man. She liked how it felt.

A slow smile spread across her face. "Are you blushing, Carter?" His skin was too dark to tell, but she could see that he was warm.

Carter found his voice. It was gruff. "That kiss would make the devil himself blush."

"But you liked it?" Anna asked.

Carter coughed a quick laugh. "Yes, little girl, you could say that." Gone was his soft expression. It was replaced by something much more intense. Adoration or maybe savagery—she couldn't tell.

She continued to grin at him.

"Wipe that smirk off your face and get on the horse," he growled.

Anna stood in place. She wasn't done reveling in her newfound power. She had never seen Carter flustered in this way, and it emboldened her. "I forget," she said, her tone saucy, "Was that kiss supposed to make me remember something?"

His voice lowered even more. "You're in so much trouble, angel. You have no idea the wicked things I'm going to do to you someday."

She knew he was talking about things that happened between a man and his wife. She smiled even wider. He wanted to marry her. She was almost certain of this. Of course! He wouldn't have kissed her otherwise. She felt like she was going to burst any moment with the strong feelings welling up inside of her.

She stepped on the block and slid her foot in the stirrup. When she was seated on Bella, Carter handed her the reins. She walked a few steps forward until Carter told her to stop. Moving to her side, he adjusted the stirrup so it was the right length for her height. He grabbed her ankle and shoved her foot into the correctly lengthened stirrup. He moved to the other side and matched the length in that stirrup. He manhandled that foot in place as well.

"The stirrups only need to be adjusted once, unless someone else rides her," he said, his voice rough.

They walked to the circular corral. Carter stood in the center with his arms crossed while Anna walked Bella around him. Carter observed her first loop in silence, then began instructing her, his voice and demeanor back to normal. "Put your heels down as much as you can. Bring the reins in a bit—there's too much slack."

Anna adjusted and rounded Carter once again. "Straighten your back and hold your head in the air. Pretend I just threatened a spanking again and you're going to tell me off."

Anna laughed. "Don't make me laugh! I'm trying to concentrate."

Carter chuckled. "Don't forget to keep your

heels down. They went up when you put your shoulders back."

He was enjoying this, Anna thought. She had shown him some sauce and he was letting her know who was in charge by mentioning the spanking and correcting every little thing she did in the saddle. The funny thing was she enjoyed it too. A lot. Carter continued to give directions while she adjusted her seat according to his instructions, which bordered on excessive. She rode for a half hour, walking and trotting Bella in circles going both directions.

Heading back to the cabin, Carter said, "You're a solid rider, Anna. You have a balanced seat and you'll be fine going back and forth from here to your place. I'll still give you a quick lesson every morning until you're as good as any saddle slicker."

Anna touched his arm and stopped. Carter stopped too and turned to face her.

Her emotions were raw. "Carter, I just want you to know…" She choked a little, unsure how to express herself. She looked past him for a moment, then turned her eyes to meet his. "I'm glad I came to work for you all those months ago."

Carter gave her braid a familiar tug. "I'm glad too, honey."

CHAPTER TEN

In the next few days, Anna developed a fascination with Carter's hands, which she imagined touching her body. She watched how he used his knife to cut his food. She watched him measure the coffee out to brew. She watched him pack tobacco into his pipe. She liked the way he lit a match and extinguished it with two flicks of the wrist. His hands were callused and skilled. It made her weak watching the way he used them.

Carter didn't kiss her again, which left her with painful longing, and when Saturday morning rolled around and he left for the range with no mention of the spanking, Anna reasoned with great disappointment and a small amount of relief that he'd forgotten. He returned that evening holding one of his saddles and an oily rag. After they'd eaten, Carter sat in his armchair with the saddle in his lap. She became mesmerized watching his hand work oil into the saddle's leather with the strip of cloth. He used rhythmic circular strokes over and over. Some time passed without her realizing. When she finally looked around, the sun had gone down and Paddy was asleep on the sofa.

"I'm going home now," she said.

Carter didn't look up. "All right, honey. Give me just a minute to finish."

"You don't have to come. I'll be fine. There's a full moon out." Anna knew what she was doing. Trying to go home alone in the dark was one of the reckless behaviors he had threatened to spank her for. She was testing him to see if he'd really punish her.

Carter continued to rub the saddle. Anna thought she saw a smile playing on his lips, but she couldn't be sure. If it was there, it was gone a second later.

Before long, he put the saddle aside, walked to the basin, and washed his hands. He dried each finger slowly and deliberately. After throwing the towel to the side, he hung his thumbs on his belt loops and leaned one of his shoulders against the wall.

"Come here, Anna."

Anna's stomach lurched. He had passed her test, and suddenly she felt very, very nervous. She trudged to him.

When she stood in front of him, he asked, "Do you remember what I said to you about reckless behavior, which includes going home alone in the dark?"

Anna knew this was her one and only chance to back out. If she apologized and said she had forgotten, he would let it go and take her home, but if she admitted to remembering and still suggesting it, he would punish her.

Anna nodded slowly. "I remember. I just don't think it's a big problem for me to walk home." She searched his face in an attempt to read his mood. Was he angry at her answer? He didn't look it. She continued to search his face, looking for a sign of the tenderness he'd shown toward her before, but she couldn't find that either. He wore a neutral expression.

"Then it looks like you're in for that spanking I promised you. Let's take a trip to the barn."

Anna's felt like her heart had crashed into her stomach. Carter picked up a lit oil lamp, opened the front door, and waited for her to pass. She wondered if this wasn't the most foolish thing she had ever put in motion, but she knew it was too late to back out. She walked past him through the door and headed toward the barn, feeling more scared with every step.

Carter hung the lamp on a nail, and the barn glowed with soft yellow light. She watched as he pulled a crate down to the ground from the top of the stack, pushed it into place with his boot tip, and took a seat. Tuck nickered at them, and for a moment Anna felt embarrassed that Tuck was going to witness this. She let out a nervous giggle when she realized how ridiculous that was.

Carter was rolling his right shirtsleeve to above his elbow. He glanced up at her. "Best not to laugh before punishment, Anna."

"I wasn't."

Carter shook his head. "It's best not to tell lies before punishment either. Now get over my lap."

She took a deep breath. She wanted this, she reminded herself, though she couldn't recall why at that very moment. With Carter's guidance, she laid herself across his hard thighs and scooted into a comfortable position. She was glad he couldn't see her face, which she was positive was the color of a tomato. Her braids hung down and the ends touched the dust and hay on the ground. Carter anchored his left hand around her waist and settled his right hand on her bottom. His hands on her body sent desire coursing through her. How could she want something so much and be so afraid at the same time?

She didn't have time to think about it. Carter brought his hand down and gave her a sound swat. He did it again, a bit harder. He applied seven more swats before he stopped. She remained quiet and motionless.

"Have you ever been punished with a spanking before, Anna?"

"No, sir," she said.

"I didn't think so. I'm not sure you would have suggested it otherwise."

Anna shifted in his lap. "I can't remember why I wanted you to do this. I, I feel scared," she stammered.

"That's natural. You should feel a little scared." He gave her a firm pat. "But you don't have too much to worry about. Now if being adorable was wrong, you'd be in for a real thrashing. You wouldn't sit for a week."

Anna's stomach fluttered.

Carter gave her another spank. "And if being a good kisser was a sin, I'd strap you with my belt until you begged for mercy. And then I would whip you harder."

Anna felt a tremor go through her, thinking about him handling her in such a harsh way. She knew he never would, but the fact that he had that power excited her.

"I'm going to lift your skirt. These layers won't let you feel a thing, and I want to make sure you feel your punishment."

Anna's body stiffened and she felt alarmed as he pushed her skirt and petticoat over her hips. Then she felt embarrassed, knowing he was looking at her bare bottom. Her three sets of drawers were in the to-be-washed pile.

"I take it you don't like wearing drawers?" he asked. "It's just as well."

Anna thought she heard mockery in his voice, and she felt worse than embarrassed. She felt humiliated. No man had ever seen her naked, and for him to laugh at her nakedness was unbearable. She felt angry and more vulnerable than ever before. "Don't laugh," she exclaimed, and tried to get up.

His grip around her tightened. "Where in tarnation do you think you're going, Miss Brown?"

The next thing she knew, her bare bottom was receiving a volley of fast, stinging swats. She yelped in surprise and forgot about her anger and humiliation. She could only think of the sting building with every swat.

He stopped as suddenly as he started. "I wasn't laughing at you, Anna." He planted a tempered but firm slap on the back of her thigh.

"Ow!"

"That's for thinking me to be a lesser man than I am. You should know me better."

"I'm sorry."

"I'm glad to hear it. That's the right attitude. Now, you said you can't remember why you wanted this punishment. I'm going to tell you what I think, and you tell me if I'm right.

She nodded and he gave her another spank.

"For months, I didn't notice you. I didn't notice the kind, beautiful woman who quietly took care of me and my son with no desire for anything other than to be noticed. Am I right about that?"

Anna nodded.

"I'd prefer if you answered out loud."

"Yes, sir."

"Thank you." He continued to spank her in

a rhythmic way, first the left cheek then the right. "You wanted me to notice you because that would mean I cared about you. Am I still on the right track?"

"Yes."

His hand came down again with more force. "You've done a few things to displease me. You want me to spank you because ignoring your misdeeds implies that I don't notice or care."

Anna couldn't believe how well he understood her feelings. He understood them better than she did.

"Did I get all of that right?"

"Yes, sir."

"In that case, young lady, you're about to learn just how much I care about you because I'm going to punish you for putting yourself in harm's way on several occasions." He raised his voice a notch. "You're never going to be reckless again, unless you want to find yourself in this same position. Do you understand?"

"Yes, sir."

Carter spanked her then without speaking. His hand came down again and again at a medium, steady tempo. After a few minutes he stopped.

"Why won't I tolerate your reckless behavior, Anna?"

"I don't know," she whimpered. She felt the sting of the spanking now. "It hurts, Carter."

He resumed spanking her. "You're getting punished, so it's supposed to hurt. And you do know why I won't tolerate it because I told you not five minutes ago. Not answering my question will only make it worse for you."

Carter continued at a faster pace with firm swats that were not very hard but that built up a sting when layered on top of each other. She squirmed on his lap and let out small noises of protest. He slowed and the swats became harder. "This is for telling me you wanted to walk home in the dark. This is for disobeying my order to rest the other day. And now, I'll ask you again. Do you know why I won't tolerate your reckless behavior?" He paused to listen.

Anna groaned. She knew the right answer was "yes," followed by the explanation that it was because he cared about her, but she was embarrassed to say it. It felt strange to be the one to say it. She also felt that the spanking might end as soon as she answered the question correctly, and she wasn't ready for it to end. She couldn't understand why being over his lap and vulnerable to pain was exactly what she wanted, but she knew she wanted to feel Carter's power and for him to truly punish her. She wanted to see just how far he would take it, and she wanted to put her trust completely in his hands.

"No, I don't know," she said in answer to his question.

For an awful moment, there was no

sound or movement at all. Carter seemed to be considering what to do. It didn't take him long to decide. His voice held heat. "Your answer is no, is it?" Carter planted a stinging swat on her untouched thigh. "That's the wrong answer, Anna, and you know it. Are you testing me?" Carter gave the same thigh another smack that made Anna's eyes moisten for the first time since being over his lap.

"You've chosen an odd time to be stubborn. Sounds to me like you need your bottom to be a whole lot sorer than I'd originally intended." The swats rained down hard and fast.

"And believe me, I'm more than willing to blister your bottom if that's what you need. Is that what you need, young lady?"

He ignored her protests and denials as he collected her wandering wrist in his left hand, pinned it to her side, and held her body tight against his. She couldn't move an inch.

He leaned over and said his next words close to her ear, "You're being disciplined. This isn't a game, and I won't tolerate acting like it is. Do you hear me? You're about to learn a very painful lesson about what happens when you misbehave over my lap."

He punished her then, the swats different from before. Every spank was solid, severe, and followed by another without pause. Five landed one on top of the other where her left cheek met her thigh. He applied the same punishment to her right cheek. She screamed for him to stop after the first two painful strokes then let out a long wail that lasted throughout the rest.

After the tenth swat, he stopped and asked for a third time, "Why won't I tolerate your reckless behavior?" His grip on her remained firm.

Anna burst into tears. She had never felt anything like what she had just experienced. It was painful and it was scary. She hadn't known when he would stop, and it seemed possible that he never would because her wail had done nothing to slow him. Her tears now didn't seem to move him either. Looking back to see his hand poised to spank again if she answered incorrectly, she felt renewed fear.

"Because you care about me," she choked through her tears and looked back down, cringing and hoping that he wouldn't bring his hand down again.

"What was that?"

"Because you care about me," Anna cried, a bit louder.

"That's right, Anna Brown. And because you made me ask three times, you're going to say it again for a third time. Very loudly, or you're going to get a repeat of what just happened." Carter reinforced his threat with another punishing swat.

"Because you care about me!" Anna sobbed. One of the horses whinnied.

"And when you're over my lap being

disciplined, how are you going to answer my questions from now on? Honestly or dishonestly?"

"Honestly."

"I hope so. Have you entered Tuck's stall again after our discussion?"

Anna gasped. The question took her by surprise and she hesitated for far too long. Her heart sank. Her hesitation would be proof enough that she had disobeyed, so it would be foolish for her to lie to him on top of it. She cried, knowing whatever she said guaranteed a round of swats that would set her roasted buns on fire even worse than they were.

"Only once," she whimpered, which was the truth.

"Only once..." he repeated slowly, sounding amazed.

As she knew it would, the punishment continued in a most painful way. The swats were hard, deliberate, and applied to every inch of her bottom. She wailed anew when he applied his hard hand to her thighs.

"Oh Carter, please!" she screamed.

"Oh Carter, please *what*? Please punish my disobedient backside in a most severe manner? Unless those were the words you planned to say, hobble your lip and accept your punishment. I should take my belt to you."

Anna accepted the rest of her punishment for visiting Tuck without speaking. She sobbed and cried out but didn't utter another word. Finally his hand settled. He released her wrist and waist from his grip and rubbed some of the sting out of her bottom. Her thighs trembled.

She thought the spanking was over. It had been long and hard and so painful that she thought it couldn't be anything except complete. She reached back to rub a place where it was smarting.

"Hold your horses, young lady. We're not quite done here." Carter took her wrist and moved it up her back, then held her hand as he planted a few more sound swats on her punished bottom. She winced. How could he not be finished? She knew he wasn't cruel, but he was acting the opposite of gentle. Perhaps he didn't know how punished and remorseful she felt.

"Please, Carter," she said through her tears. "I can't take anymore. I'm sorry for not answering your question. I'm even sorrier for visiting Tuck. I have learned my lesson. Please, can't it be over now?"

Carter responded in a voice that was firm, "I know you're sorry and that it hurts, Anna, but we're not finished. Another thing you must learn today is that you don't get to decide when your punishment is over."

Anna moaned and Carter continued to hold the wandering hand that he'd moved up her back. He caressed her fingers with his thumb and didn't spank her for a while, letting her calm down. Her soft cries were the only sounds in the barn until he spoke again, his voice still stern.

"We're going to continue. Be a good girl and it will be over soon. Do you think you can be good for me and accept the last of your punishment?"

Anna sniffled. "Yes, sir."

"That's my girl. I'm going to continue holding your hand in mine. I'm here to support you even as I am punishing you, and I hope you know I will hold all of you when we're done."

"All right," she whimpered. To her amazement, the handholding offered her considerable reassurance for the rest of the spanking. It provided a suggestion of the comfort she would soon receive.

He squeezed her hand gently and resumed the spanking, half as hard as before, but still igniting a fire on her sore backside. "I only have one more thing to discuss with you, and it's important. Although I thought it unwise when you ran all the way into my arms after getting hurt, instead of going home, you made something very clear to me." He gave her three hard swats that made Anna cry out. He continued to spank her before her cries ceased.

"That day you chose to make me responsible for taking care of you and protecting you, didn't you, Anna?"

"Yes, sir," she gasped.

"I take that responsibility seriously. I want you to be mine, and I always protect what's mine."

The final four swats were firm and measured between pauses. "Protecting you includes disciplining you when you choose to be reckless. When you disobey. And when you don't take your discipline seriously." He landed a final swat. "Have I made myself quite clear on all accounts tonight, young lady?"

"Yes," Anna moaned, the word leaving her mouth slowly in misery.

"Then we're finished." Carter folded her skirt back over her bottom.

Anna hung over his legs and cried. When her cries settled a bit, she said, "I'll never do anything to earn another spanking like that. Never, ever, ever."

Carter gathered her into a hug on his lap. "I almost believe that. You're a good girl." He wiped away the tears on her cheek and tucked a piece of hair that escaped her braid behind her ear. "I know you feel I was hard on you, but that spanking won't hurt past tonight." He cuddled her into him and stroked her back, his hands now gentle and comforting.

Anna buried her face in the curve of his neck and shoulder and basked in his comfort for some time. When she found her normal voice, she made a three-word declaration that made his hand freeze on her back mid-rub. "You love me."

Carter was silent a moment before he let out a long, soft chuckle. "Anna, you are the most transparent woman I've ever met, yet you surprise me." He sighed. "This isn't exactly when or how I wanted to say it to you the first time, but yes, I do love you. I'd have to be crazy or dead not to love you."

"I love you too," Anna said.

"That's obvious, honey. Quite obvious. But I thank you for saying it."

CHAPTER ELEVEN

It was the morning after the spanking, and Carter dawdled in the cabin for some time before leaving for work. He didn't want to focus on anything but Anna's beautiful, glowing face. She glanced shyly at him all morning, smiling more than he'd ever seen her smile. He smiled back when he caught her eye. The spanking had been just what she needed to understand that he cared about her, and it had been just what he needed to establish the kind of relationship they would have. He was a man good at taking charge, and she was a woman who thrived off his authority.

Anna sat at the table for a spell after washing the dishes and asked for a cup of coffee, which Carter served to her. He sat down with his own cup and watched her make a face when she took her first sip.

He smiled. "It's an acquired taste, love. Much like whiskey. You know something about that, don't you?"

Anna's cheeks grew pink. "You called me 'love'," she said. She twirled a braid in between her fingers.

"I did. Stop blushing, love."

She blushed harder, and he chuckled. "You haven't already forgotten what happens when you disobey, have you?"

Anna's eyes widened and she protested. "That's not fair. I can't help what my face does."

"I know," he said, grinning.

Anna slapped him lightly on his arm and he caught her wrist. There were two drops of water on her hand leftover from washing the dishes. He kissed each drop.

"I like your hands," he said. "They're so small."

"I like yours too. They're...not small."

"No, they're not." He grinned devilishly. "I wager I can wrap one of my hands around both of your wrists." He clasped her two hands together. His thumb and middle finger trapped her wrists in the handcuff of his making. Anna looked at her captured hands, blushing furiously. He released her.

"I've got to stop teasing you so often, but you make it hard. You're adorable when you blush."

Anna took a sip of coffee and made another face. "You're not nice."

"No," he agreed. "Nice wouldn't be a good description of me."

"In fact you're most disagreeable," she asserted.

"Am I? I suppose I agree. Yes, I will agree that I am disagreeable," he said, winking at her. Anna caught the irony and giggled.

Paddy wandered over and climbed onto Carter's lap. Carter wrapped him in his arms and squeezed him, then growled and attacked him with a few rough kisses that made Paddy squeal and jerk around in his arms. "Stop it, Pa! Your beard hurts."

Carter ran a hand over his face. "Sorry, little man. Pa needs a scrape."

"Yes, you do," Paddy said in a very serious voice.

Anna and Carter laughed. Carter rested his chin on the top of his son's head and looked at Anna. This was one of those perfect moments in life, he realized. The two people he loved most were within arm's length. Anna smiled at him, and he took her hand. Her eyes were wet, and he knew she felt the same.

The time had come for him to court her properly so that he could ask her to marry him. Carter no longer wanted her to work for him. He felt the desire to work for her. He hadn't kissed her again because it didn't feel right for him to take such liberties while she wasn't being properly courted. The respectable thing would be to visit her, bring her a gift, take her out for the evening, and leave her with a chaste kiss goodbye. Kissing how they had was scandalous before marriage. He had no qualms about it, but he wanted to protect her from the tongue-wagging that would happen if anyone caught them doing such a thing.

He observed the woman before him choking down the last of her coffee, and his heart swelled with the feeling of his particular love for her. His love for her was different, but just as strong, as his love had been for Nalin. He found it difficult to understand how it could be that the only two women he ever loved were such opposites. With Nalin, he'd been constantly challenged, on his toes, and working to keep her happy. She was exciting, and she baffled and enlightened him with her ideas about women voting and having a say in politics. Everything about her demanded respect, and he gave it to her in heaps.

Anna was too shy to be demanding. Her fragility and innocence brought out in him a need to protect her at all costs. She was strong in her own way, but her strength in relation to him rested in her ability to lower his guard and soften him. One of the ways she did this was by subjecting him to her candor at will and without warning.

Paddy slid off Carter's lap and announced that he was going to collect eggs from the henhouse, his new favorite chore. As soon as the door closed behind him, Anna turned to Carter and frowned. "Carter, did you spank your wife?"

Carter choked on the coffee he was in the midst of swallowing and coughed a few times. "I cannot believe you just asked me that."

"You said I could talk to you about sensitive matters, including Nalin," she reminded him coolly. "I need to know."

"Why the devil do you need to know?"

"Because I need to know if you love me romantically like you loved your wife."

Her frank words brought his outrage to a dizzying halt and left him with a headache. He rubbed his forehead before moving his hand to rub the back of his neck. "Anna, your feelings are undisguised and on the surface, whereas mine need to climb through a few layers of tough skin. Can you not give me the chance to first to tell you how I feel about you before you insist that I speak of it?"

Her frown deepened. He was certain she had no idea what he was talking about. To her, this topic required no artfulness, much like when she informed him that he loved her after he finished paddling her behind. She'd also informed him a few days ago that he found her pretty. Of all the cheek!

"Well? Did you spank her or not?" Her voice was insistent.

Carter groaned. He wasn't going to be able to avoid answering this question. He set his coffee down on the table. "I'll put it this way. I reckon most days there wasn't a woman in all of Texas who had a more blistered behind than my brazen biddy, nor was there ever a woman who deserved or craved it more."

Anna's face broke into a happy smile. "Thank you, Carter. That's all I needed to know."

"I'm glad my answer pleases you," he grunted and then scowled. "If it please you further, permit me to express additional sentiments about your beauty and my love for you and any romantic inclinations I might have, without your prodding. I would like to do it on my own, sweet, cottonpickin' time! Though truly, I don't know how much else you've left me to say."

"There is the matter of a marriage propos—"

"Enough!" he shouted, jumping to his feet. He pointed a finger at her. "Not another word, little girl. I mean it. Don't think I won't turn you over my knee right now if you speak of that further. I might just spank you anyway."

"I'm sorry," she said, focusing her big green eyes at him. They twinkled at what was surely in her opinion an amusing overreaction from him.

"Very well," he said wearily. He sat back down.

After a minute, they were back to smiling at each other like two lovesick puppies. Watching her twirl her braid, he realized something. He'd never seen her hair fashioned in any other way, just two straight braids down the front of her dress. He wondered how she would look with her long blonde hair flowing freely around her head.

"When are you going to stop wearing those braids? Aren't you getting a little old for them?"

Anna stopped twirling and frowned thoughtfully. "I think they look nice. But I'll stop braiding when I get married. When I get married I won't care if I look nice because I'll have already hooked a man. I'll wear my hair in a knot and get fat off candy."

Carter laughed. He couldn't stop. As soon as he thought he had control, he would lose it again. Anna smiled, looking pleased with herself.

"You're such a strange girl," he said when he could breathe. "Is that a test to see if I scare off easily?"

"No, I just wanted to make you laugh."

"Good job, darlin'. You did quite well with that. Just so as you know, I'd love you just as much and find you just as beautiful with more meat on your delicious bones."

Anna's face lit up. She sighed. "Oh, Carter. That was so nice of you to say."

"See? Doesn't it feel better when my words catch you by surprise and are not delivered at your request?

She blinked at him. She twirled her braid around and seemed to be considering his words, but then she said, "What about if I wore my hair in a knot? Would you still find me beautiful then?"

Carter let out a long, frustrated groan. Without a word, he strode out of the cabin before he spanked her for being so guileless and too damn cute.

* * *

Anna had confirmed that Carter was sweet on her, and she wondered when he would propose. It seemed like he was waiting for something, and she didn't understand what. The days passed. Her stomach fluttered every time she saw him. She loved him more than she thought it was possible to love anyone and yearned to be with him in a physical way. He held back from touching or kissing her, and Anna grew hungry for his caress. She wanted his hands and lips on every part of her body. She knew that he'd no doubt spank her again if she did something deserving of it, and the thought of him spanking her made her feel nervous and aroused. Still, she didn't want to incite him to anger just to get a spanking. She wanted him to desire her enough to touch her.

Going about her days with her head in the clouds, she wasn't prepared for the sudden hardship that life delivers to people in various cruel ways. For Anna it arrived in the form of a man on the doorstep. It was in the early afternoon while Carter and his men were out driving cattle to a greener pasture. Anna sat on the floor of the cabin playing with Paddy. She helped him build a house with the new wood blocks that Carter had bought from town. The door swung open and a man stormed in. Anna recognized him from the restaurant where Carter had taken her for her birthday. He was one of Carter's ranch hands, Joe, the man who had laughed at her. Her first thought upon seeing him was that Carter was hurt.

"What is it?" she gasped, her hand covering her mouth as if to stifle a scream. "Did something happen?"

The look Joe gave her made her shiver. "Oh, yeah, something happened all right. The boss refused me a raise after all the work I've done for him. Seems he's fixin' to get rid of me too after this drive."

Anna felt relief that Carter wasn't hurt, but it was quickly replaced by fear. She saw the rage in Joe's eyes. She smelled the whiskey on his breath from three meters away.

"I-I'm sorry, but I can't do anything about that. Carter doesn't discuss the affairs of his ranch with me."

He took a step toward her. "No? I thought you were his *employee*."

She knew he was mocking her, but she wasn't angry. She was afraid, and she stayed quiet. She didn't like the way his eyes roamed her body, and Paddy didn't seem to like the man either. He climbed into her lap where she was seated cross-legged on the floor. She put her arms about him protectively.

"Maybe you're more than his servant girl. He

did take you to supper. Some of us are of the mind that he's having his way with you whenever he likes. Maybe that's the kind of work you do. Are you a strumpet?"

"I don't get your meaning," Anna said, fear creeping up her spine.

Joe laughed a cruel laugh. "You don't even paint yourself. What kind of a whore are you?"

"I'm not any kind of whore. I am a respectable farmer's daughter and a respectable rancher's employee. Both would be offended if I told them of your obscenity, as am I. What do you want?"

"Good question. I want to make the *respectable* rancher suffer, one way or another. Somehow I think that includes harassing his little slewer. It didn't escape me that he feels it's his sworn duty to defend your honor. I wonder how he'd like it if I took it and gave him a taste of humble pie."

Anna held Paddy closer to her. "I've got to get this little one down for a nap, Joe. Perhaps you could come for a visit another time."

Joe laughed again. She felt a desperate need to escape, but it didn't seem possible. Joe was in front of the door. She might be able to get herself and Paddy to the bedroom before Joe got there, but he'd reach them before they'd be able to climb through the window. Next, Anna considered weapons. Without looking around, she made list in her mind. The poker was only a step away at the fireplace's hearth. A knife was in the kitchen drawer. Anna swallowed and told herself fiercely that she was to be brave and not cry.

"Send the brat to bed so we can have a nice little chat."

Anna forced herself to smile agreeably. "That's not a bad idea. Paddy, you be good for me and go to the bedroom. Don't come out until I say. All right, sweetie?"

"All right, Miss Anna." She lifted him to his feet in front of her, and he walked to the bedroom. She watched his retreat with an aching heart. They were both in danger if Joe wanted to make Carter suffer in a big way, and she had to find a way out of it.

"Close the door behind you, sweetheart," Anna called to him. Paddy did so and Anna turned her focus to Joe. She scrambled out of her position on the floor and stood. Doing her best to sound calm and breezy, she said, "Can I make you some coffee, Joe?"

"Sure, sweetheart. You do that." He sat in the middle of the sofa. He spread his arms across the back and opened his legs wide, unconcerned with manners in her presence.

Hearing him sneer the word "sweetheart" disgusted Anna. She moved to the kitchen and lit the fire. She opened the drawer and picked up a spoon, making a note of the knife. She slowly spooned coffee into the pot and estimated in her head how long it would be before Carter returned.

She realized with growing panic it wouldn't be for some time. Occasionally, he would be home as early as an hour from then. Usually it was at least three hours. On two occasions he'd shown up around the current hour, but the first time it was because the weather had taken a turn, and the second time it was when he needed one of his mares from the barn to set up a new cowhand. That was the day he found her with Tuck.

Anna tried to steady her shaking hand as she poured the brewed coffee into a mug. Everything felt very wrong. She had never felt so scared in the presence of a man. She held the coffee out to Joe, standing as far away from him as possible while handing it over.

He took it and drank a gulp. He looked at her with revulsion. "This is almost as bad as the black water Carter makes at camp."

Anna sat on the edge of the armchair across from where Joe was seated. "Joe, after you've had your coffee, I think you ought to leave. Carter won't be happy to hear I've entertained a guest while he's away." This wasn't true, but she hoped bringing Carter's name back into the room would offer some authority to the conversation that she didn't possess.

It didn't work. Joe's face twisted scornfully. "Of course you're going to cry to him and tell him you *entertained*, aren't you? That's fine by me. You'll tell him every last thing I do to you, but my name won't come out of your mouth if you want to live to your next birthday."

Anna's panic grew. Her voice became more insistent. "Joe, I would like you to leave. I have a lot of work to do."

"Yes, you do." Joe set the coffee mug on the table next to the sofa with a bang, causing some of it to splash out. "First you're going to suck me." He made a lewd gesture between his spread legs before he stood up and released the button on his trousers. Anna felt terror wash over her. She couldn't keep the tears back after the confirmation that her instinct had been right.

"Joe, leave now," Anna begged.

Joe lunged at her. He grabbed her by the arms as she screamed. "That wasn't a very polite thing to say," he snarled.

"Stop. Please!"

He threw her to the floor and straddled her. He grasped at the collar of her dress and tore it, exposing the top of one of her breasts.

"I'm going to show you how to be polite to a man. Seems no one has trained you properly."

Anna's heart broke into pieces at the next words that filled the room. They weren't from Joe.

"Miss Anna, are you all right?" Paddy stood in the frame of the bedroom door.

"Yes! Go back in the room, Paddy."

Joe turned to the scared little boy. "Why, you little shit! Didn't feel like listening to instructions, did you? First I'll teach you a lesson, then I'll teach the bitch hers." He moved toward the child.

"Leave him alone," Anna shrieked, scrambling to her feet.

Joe continued in Paddy's direction. Anna grabbed the poker by the hearth and brought it down as hard as she could as Joe grabbed Paddy by the collar. The blow was on his shoulder, and it wasn't as hard as it needed to be. Like an injured grizzly, it only enraged and empowered him.

Snarling and still holding Paddy in the air by his shirt, he backhanded Anna, sending her to the floor. He grabbed the poker and raised it in the air to strike her. Anna screamed and covered her face with her arms.

That was the scene Carter opened the door to find—Joe holding his son roughly by the collar and Anna screaming on the floor, cowering in anticipation of being struck.

Through the fog of her terror, Anna heard Carter's voice yell a phrase she would never have imagined him using in her presence, "What the *fuck*?" It filled Anna with more relief than she'd ever known. Joe dropped Paddy and the poker at the same time and made a run for it.

Anna heard the sound of scuffling and a fist connecting with bones as she crawled to the stunned child on the floor. Gathering Paddy into her arms, she said in his ear, "Your pa's here now, baby. Everything will be all right." She held his face against her chest so that he wouldn't be able to see what was happening. Still on the floor, she pivoted around on her knees. Carter was smashing his fist into Joe's face. Joe slumped and fell to the floor. He was either knocked out or dead, and Anna didn't much care which. Blood covered Joe's face and Carter's knuckles.

Carter rushed to Paddy and Anna. After wiping some of Joe's blood off his hand onto his shirt, he picked up Paddy, whose arms were outstretched to him. Carter looked him over. "Are you hurt, son?"

Paddy only cried.

"He's not hurt. You got here in time," Anna said. Still on her knees, she put her face in her hands, trying to settle her sobs. She heard a tormented noise escape from Carter's throat, and the next thing she knew she was being carried. One of Carter's arms was under her back, the other under her legs. Carter sat on the sofa with her in his lap and hugged her to him. Paddy sat next to them. He leaned into his father, and Carter wrapped an arm around him.

"Oh, honey," he said to Anna, his voice sounding devastated. He moved the torn piece of her dress to cover the exposed part of her breast. "Can you tell me what happened?"

Anna held a hand to her chest to hold the piece of fabric in place and shifted to sit next to him while Paddy took her place in his lap. Carter reached to take her free hand. She looked down at his bloody fist.

In a monotone, shaky voice, she related the events of the afternoon. The whole time she spoke, she looked down at Carter's hand. She told him every small detail because her mind wasn't working well enough to filter out what was important and what wasn't. Her shocked state prevented her from giving an orderly timeline of events, so she skipped around and Carter had to figure out the order for himself. He didn't interrupt once, only listened. She explained how many spoons of coffee grounds she used to make Joe's coffee in the same way that she explained how he had backhanded her. She repeated Joe's words about the rumor that she was Carter's whore. She told him how high Paddy stacked the blocks and about her mental list of weapons. Every word from Joe's mouth came out of hers in the same lazy fashion, even the word he used to describe her as a female dog. When she was finished telling Carter everything that happened, she looked over at him.

He was shaking and looking at the ground. Joe moaned in the corner and tried to get off the floor. His attempt was unsuccessful and he slumped back down.

"Anna," Carter said, his voice as shaky as hers had been. He looked at her. "You were so brave, my love. So very brave."

Anna wiped the back of her hand under her eye to remove some tears. "It wouldn't have made a lick of difference if you hadn't shown up, Carter. Why did you come back so early? I thought you wouldn't be home for hours. It would have ended badly."

Carter grimaced. "I can't bear to think of it. I came back because I couldn't find that bastard," he said, looking at Joe. "He wasn't with my men in the pasture." He stopped short. "I'm sorry, Anna. I don't wish to curse in front of you or my little man here." Carter bent and gave Paddy a kiss on the top of his head.

Anna laughed without humor. "I don't care, Carter. Really."

"I thought Joe may have injured himself on the ride out without anyone noticing. I also knew he was sore at me, so part of me worried he was up to something, though I never imagined..." Carter sucked in a breath. "I returned to the bunkhouse without seeing him and decided that while I was around, I might as well ride the mile out to see you and Paddy."

Joe cried out and sat up with some success before he fell back over. Carter stared at him, still shaking.

"I'll never forgive myself for this. I knew he was rough, but I didn't know... I should have known! You being employed here made you prey to men with leaky mouths repeating obscene things about you. You! Of all people! Our arrangement wasn't proper after people saw us at the restaurant together. I'll never forgive myself for letting you work here after that."

"Carter, you didn't do anyth—"

"I did. By allowing your employment to

continue after that day, I allowed this to happen. You don't understand."

Carter was right. She didn't understand. She didn't understand at all, and she felt like the incident with Joe had ruined everything. The way that Carter was speaking, it sounded like he regretted all of the months she'd worked for him and all of their wonderful moments together.

Carter looked for some time at Joe, still shaking with rage, then cleared his throat and locked eyes with Anna. "I need your help right now. Can you help me with something?"

"I'll do anything, Carter. What do you need?" Anna reached over and touched his cheek, which was rough with its usual stubble. The look in his eyes scared her. She saw anger and remorse, but also something else, desperation.

"I need you to tell me not to kill him. Because if you don't, I'm going to."

Anna wrapped her arms around his neck. She bent her head to his ear and said, "Don't kill him, Carter. He's not worth it. Take him to the marshal."

He held her face in his hands and gave her a short, tender kiss. "Thank you, angel."

His words and kiss comforted her. Maybe he didn't regret their time together after all.

CHAPTER TWELVE

Carter tied Joe onto a horse and walked him to the marshal, while Anna rode home on Bella. The following day was Sunday, Anna's day off, and he felt relieved that she would be safe with her parents while he made arrangements. Carter told her she was to go to church with them and not stay home alone. Anna agreed without argument, though he knew she hated church.

During the day that she was away, he asked Grace if she'd mind Paddy at her and Ben's cabin while he tended to the ranch, and she agreed. Now he could end Anna's employment, once and for all, and move forward with his plan to court and marry her.

Monday morning, Carter awaited Anna's arrival by standing on the porch outside. He leaned against a beam with a mug of coffee in his hand. He spotted her on Bella trotting toward his place down the path, and he felt pride watching her confident and skilled movements on horseback. Anna waved to him and slowed to a walk. She entered the barn still seated on Bella's back.

Minutes later she strutted toward the house. She wore the split-skirt riding outfit he'd bought for her and a cowboy hat she'd bought for herself. She was the prettiest cowgirl he'd ever seen.

"Hello, buckaroo. You're looking mighty fine on that horse."

"Thank you, cowboy," she said, climbing the porch stairs to him. She was a bit winded and her voice was breathy. "I'm getting better and better. Next you must teach me to ride a canter well. I want to go faster."

"Definitely. All in good time."

Anna removed her hat, revealing her unshaded flushed face and the top of her blonde head.

"You're such a beauty, Anna."

"Thank you," she said, flashing him a smile.

Carter splashed the remaining cold coffee from his mug onto the dirt. "I need to talk to you about something. Let's go inside."

They settled on the sofa, and Carter got right to the point. "I've decided it's time to end your employment. You're not to be here anymore as my employee. I will visit you at your parents' farm."

Anna's jaw dropped. "But I don't want to stop

coming here. I like it here."

"I'm glad, but I want you to leave here today unburdened by chores. I want you to have the freedom to experience the better parts of life. For instance, I want you to experience what it's like to be courted by a man."

Carter watched the blood drain from her face. He frowned. "What is it? Why are you looking at me like that?"

Anna's expression went from confused to hurt to enraged in the span of a few seconds. She rose to her feet and spat her words down at him. "How could you not want me here? How could you make me think…?" A sob caught in her throat. "All those things you said…." She couldn't finish a sentence. She stormed to the front of the cabin with Carter quick at her heels.

"Whatever is wrong, Anna?" He put a hand on her shoulder, but she shook him off and ran out the door without looking at him.

Carter stood on the porch watching her retreat at a sprint. He was stunned. Why did she feel so bad about not working for him anymore? Didn't she know that her time away was temporary, since he'd said he wanted to court her? Surely she knew that meant he wanted to marry her and move her to his place for good. He shook his head, completely confused. There was no way she was that unfamiliar with how these things worked.

He wondered if he had made a grave mistake

somehow, but he couldn't for the life of him reason what it might be. A desire to give chase came over him, but he stood in one place until he convinced himself it was the right decision to send her away, even if she was upset about not being at his place for a while. He thought perhaps he should give her some time to herself, but it was clear to him that he wouldn't be able to stay away long. Even waiting a week would be torture, since after a few minutes it took everything in him to keep from running after her.

* * *

Anna ran the whole way home. By the time she arrived, her lungs were burning and she could hardly breathe. She welcomed the searing pain in her chest and side. She wanted anything to distract her from Carter's words, but his voice still boomed in her head. Nothing he'd said made sense to her. How could he want her to leave and be courted by another man? Why didn't he want her there with him and Paddy anymore? Her mind spun. She tried to think what she could have said or done to make him reject her. A murderous rage came over her. She wished she'd let Carter kill Joe. Everything had gone sour after that evil man accosted her and changed Carter's mind about her employment there.

Anna let out a wail without realizing it

and sank to her knees on the grass outside her family's cabin. She buried her face in her hands and cried like she had never cried before. Deep, uncontrollable sobs took over, and her whole body shook.

"Anna!" Paul was standing in front of her. "Anna, what happened?"

He grabbed her arms and pulled her to her feet. She continued to sob into her hands. "Oh, Pa," she said.

Paul shook her. "Tell me what's wrong. Is someone hurt?"

"No," she wailed. "It's Carter. He sent me away. He doesn't want me anymore."

"Get ahold of yourself, girl. Calm down and tell me what he said."

Anna couldn't calm herself. She cried and hung in his arms. Paul led her to the picnic table in their front yard, where she collapsed and buried her head in her arms. Anna's mother stepped out from the cabin and rushed toward them. Anna had always been a crier. She was more sensitive than most, and Margie had spent many hours comforting Anna after various minor traumas. But Anna had never cried like this.

"What happened, Paul?" she asked, fear in her voice. She sat by her daughter and put a hand on her shaking back.

"She thinks Carter sent her away," he said. "But she won't calm down long enough to explain."

"You, you don't understand," Anna

stammered. "He said things to me that made me think he wanted to.... I let him..." She felt too ashamed to continue. If her parents knew that she had let Carter kiss her without proposing to her first, they would be disappointed in her. And oh! If they knew she had been partly naked over his lap getting a spanking, how shocked and ashamed would they be? They could never know. She couldn't understand how this had happened. How had she been wrong about how he felt about her?

"I thought I knew how he felt about me," she said. She grew too weak to continue crying. She wanted only to sleep.

"What did he say?" Paul demanded.

Her sobs were gone, and left in their stead was a quiet, broken languor. Her words were quiet and devastating to her own ears. "He said he wanted me to leave and to experience what it's like to be courted. He wants me to be with another man."

Paul frowned. "I'm not sure that's what he meant. But he's as shy of brains as a horse is of feathers. That's for sure." He paused briefly before continuing. "I made a promise to Carter that I'm regretting keeping right about now. Let me ask you something. If he were to come here tomorrow and say he wanted to marry you, would you want that?"

She let out another wail. The thought about what might have been shattered her. "He won't, Pa. He regrets ever hiring me. He wanted me to leave. Those were his words. 'I want you to leave'." She gasped suddenly, remembered something else Carter had said.

"Oh, no," Anna cried again. "He said he was going to visit me here." Anxiety crept into her voice. "I don't want to see him. I can't bear the shame of looking at him. Please tell him he can't see me, Pa. Please."

"I'll tell him," Paul said.

❊ ❊ ❊

The next morning, Carter closed the barn gate after feeding the horses and turned to see Paul walking at a quick clip down the path toward him. Carter could tell something was wrong from the way he walked, but he was still unprepared for what happened. Paul came at him without slowing and punched him hard on the left side of his face.

Carter staggered back. "What in the hell?" he cursed, holding his face and scrambling to find his feet.

Paul jabbed two fingers into his chest and shoved him, nearly sending him to the ground.

"That's for breaking my little girl's heart. I have a question for you and a few things to say, and then you'll be rid of me."

Carter found his bearings and moved his hand to under his nose, which was bleeding.

"Do you still want to marry Anna, or have

you changed your mind?"

"What? I want to marry her! Of course I haven't changed my mind. I want—"

Paul held up his hand. "I know, I know. You want to court her. Of all the tomfoolery I've heard in my time, that wins the blue ribbon. Do you even know Anna? She is the most plainspoken and practical woman God put on this green earth. She needs a man who proclaims his feelings for her and makes good on them, not games and a stupid ritual! Are you a man, Carter? Or are you scared? Maybe that's the real reason you sent her away." Paul shoved him again.

Carter attempted to argue, but Paul held a finger to his bloodied face and continued. "Let me tell you something. Anna thinks you don't want her and that you want another man to court her. Whatever you said yesterday made her think that. She begged me not to allow you near her. It chafes me to go against her, but I will allow you to see her once. Once! You hear me? You have one chance to make things right before I honor her wish. How long you choose to leave her brokenhearted is up to you, but you're not to set foot on my property unless it's to beg her forgiveness and ask for her hand. And you'd better pray she hasn't written you off by the time you find the poor excuse for brains you have rattling around your head."

With that, Paul turned and strode away, leaving Carter staring after him, still holding a hand under his bloody nose.

Carter felt dizzy and ill. He stumbled up the steps to the bench on the porch and collapsed.

Paddy opened the front door and walked outside. "Pa, are you hurting?"

"I'm all right, little man. Go and fetch me some water, will you?"

Paddy disappeared and returned lugging a half-full bucket of water with all his might, spilling most of it along the way. Carter cupped water in his hands and rinsed the blood from his face. He stood. He tilted the bucket above him and drank the rest of the water. After setting the bucket down, he lifted Paddy into his arms, and Paddy rested his head on Carter's shoulder.

Carter walked inside and sat down, still holding his son against him.

"Don't be sad, Pa." Paddy's voice trembled. Carter had always kept a stiff upper lip around him, and seeing his father in this state seemed to unnerve him.

Carter pulled him away and examined his sweet face. "You look just like your mama, Patrick. I loved your ma, little man, and I love you. You know that, don't you?"

Paddy nodded. "Yes, Pa."

"Do you know who else I love?"

"Who?"

"I love Miss Anna."

"Me too. I love Miss Anna too. I think you should marry her."

Carter pulled him back in for a hug. "In that

case, Patrick, I will."

CHAPTER THIRTEEN

Carter thanked Grace for watching Paddy as he packed two decorative hair combs and a gold ring he'd bought in town into his vest pocket. He saddled Bella and set out at a canter for the neighboring farm. It had been two days since he'd seen Anna, but it felt like two lifetimes.

Carter saw her before she saw him. She was sitting at the picnic table out in front of the cabin, halfheartedly flipping through a dime novel and twirling one of her predictable braids. When Anna noticed him, she flew to her feet and closed her hands into fists at her sides. Her defensive stance irritated him. He dismounted and tied Bella to a nearby tree.

He adjusted the stirrups back to their previous length to fit Anna's height and removed the saddle from Bella's back. He walked the four strides to the table carrying the saddle in one hand by the pommel and slammed it down on the bench, which made Anna jump.

"You left your horse," Carter growled in lieu of hello. He examined her face. Her eyes were red and her cheeks were wet. Her entire face was swollen. He wondered how many hours she'd spent crying over the last two days. The bruise from Joe's backhand was visible on her face, and Carter's ire about the current situation deepened.

She noticed how rough he looked too. "What happened to your face?"

"Don't worry about it. Sit down," he said sharply and pointed to the bench across the table from him.

Anna fell onto the seat. She looked up at him, her big green eyes bloodshot and filled with sadness.

Carter felt stabs of remorse for the sorrow he saw in her eyes. It now made perfect sense to him why Paul had given him such a wallop. Seeing her like that was the worst thing in the world. He regretted not chasing her down and setting her straight the moment she ran away. All of her pain could have been avoided if he'd had the presence of mind to stop her.

He sat down across from her. His voice was hard. "Your pa told me you think I want another man to court you. That's not what I meant. I meant that *I* want to court you."

Anna blinked and stared at him vacantly.

She looked worse than tired. She looked dazed. He continued, softening his tone a bit. "I may have made a mistake asking you to leave, but I did what I thought was best for you and for us in the long run."

Anna looked down at her hands. "Maybe I know what's best for me. You didn't bother to ask me." Her bottom lip quivered, and her voice shook. He wasn't the only one angry, it seemed.

"I know, Anna, and that was wrong of me. I hope you will forgive me for that."

Anna shrugged and continued to stare at her hands.

"I have an important question to ask you, so I'd like if you could look at me."

A tear slid down her face and she glared at him with fire in her eyes. "I won't go back, if that's what you want to ask, now that I know you regret my employment and do not wish me to be there."

Carter felt like she'd slapped him. His temper flared and his jaw clenched. "Anna," he said through his teeth, struggling to keep his voice level. "I do want you there. How could you think otherwise?" He reached out and tried to take her hand. She pulled it away.

"I think otherwise because you said otherwise!" she yelled at him and slammed both palms on the table. Her bottom lip pouted pitifully before she continued. "You said that you shouldn't have employed me. You have hurt me most viciously and more than Joe ever could. You let that brute make you regret your time with me. You let him ruin everything. I wish I'd let you kill him!"

"No, angel. Don't say that. He ruined nothing, I assure you." Carter was beginning to understand.

"Then why did you say not two days prior that you no longer wanted me to work for you?"

Carter drew a few deep breaths before he rounded the table and sat next to her on the bench, facing out. He felt her body stiffen when his leg brushed her hip. That was her second recoil from his touch, and it displeased him greatly. It was foolish for her to ignore the love he'd shown her and make outlandish assumptions from words he spoke under duress.

With some difficulty, he squashed the urge to drag her to the woodshed a few yards away and give her a good paddling. Instead, he took one of her braids in his hand, carefully, as though she were a nervous filly he didn't want to spook, and rubbed it between his thumb and forefinger. "I love these silly braids," he muttered.

She sniffled. He pulled the ribbon at the end and began to unbraid it tress by tress, willing her not to pull away. She remained stiff at his side but didn't make any attempt to bolt. He finished and left that half of her hair loose down her back.

"I love everything about you," he continued. He rose to his feet and stood behind her. He unraveled her other braid slowly, still worried she might break away at any moment. While he worked on unbraiding her hair, he spoke. "I feel I have been forthright about my feelings for you, Anna, but it doesn't seem you would agree from what you've been saying to me. Listen to me now. I love you very much and I want you with me. Nothing will change that." He finished unbraiding. "My god," he breathed. Her hair cascaded in waves down her back. It was even more beautiful than he'd imagined. He gathered some of it into his hands and ran his fingers through it. Her hair's flowery scent gave him a heady feeling. Carter thought he felt her relax. "What happened with Joe terrified me. All the ways it could have been worse were on my mind. I am only a man, Anna, and a man can only lose so much in one life before he is broken. I wouldn't wish to live another day if I lost you or my son. I blamed myself for the possibility of it happening. The ways I could have prevented it ran through my mind. I thought out loud. That doesn't mean I regret a single second you've spent with me and Paddy."

He took one of the decorative combs he'd brought and fastened a piece of her hair to it. She looked ravishing. "Ending your employment and sending you away was not an action of regret." For the next part of his speech, he needed to see her face. He took her arm at the elbow and helped her to her feet. She turned to face him, tears streaming down her face. "It was a step toward our future. I wanted to court you, but courtship is no longer an option. Therefore, I'm asking you today. Will you marry me?"

Anna looked at him with love and misery combined. He reached for her hand, and this time she let him take it. Retrieving the ring from his vest, he slid it onto her finger.

"That's for you, if you'll have me as your husband," he said, and kissed her hand. "Often I worry that you'll get hurt by this cruel world. The last thing I wanted was to be the one to hurt you. Believe that. I only ever want to love and protect you for as long as I live."

She closed her eyes and two tears fell from her eyelashes. One of the tears stopped at the corner of her mouth. Carter brushed it aside, grazing her lips with his thumb when he did. Time passed.

"Talk to me, sweetheart. What are you thinking?"

She blinked away the last of her tears. "I'm thinking so many things. My mind won't stop. I'm ashamed of how much I hated you and didn't understand your intentions. I felt such pain. I couldn't think clearly. Oh, how I have I hated you these last two days."

Carter felt himself scowling. "Yes, I know. I'm not exactly in good favor with the Brown family. Your father hasn't cared for me much either, as you can see," he said, pointing to his face. Anna's eyebrows shot up. "My pa hit you? Oh, Carter! It's all my fault."

"My fault as well. I should have been clearer,

I suppose. I planned to ask for your hand soon. It wasn't going to be a long courtship, but your pa sped up the process even more because he saw what I didn't. He saw that you need a promise from me now. Do you understand?"

Anna nodded. "I love you more than anything, Carter. You're a good man for wanting to court me. I'm sorry I didn't understand the meaning of your words."

He looked into her eyes for a moment before he cupped the back of her head in his hand, entangling her hair in his fingers. He wrapped his other arm around her waist to pull her toward him. Tilting his head down, he kissed her. Anna reached around and held firm to his back. Their passion grew as they kissed. When he felt Anna growing needy and aroused in his arms, he took a generous fistful of her hair above the neck and pulled her head back, unlocking her lips from his. She whimpered.

"You like that?" he growled against her neck. He wished he could bend her over the table and take her there, hard and rough like she deserved for doubting his love. He peppered her with kisses from her collarbone up to her ear and bit her earlobe. Anna moaned and he nipped her again. He pulled her hair harder, bringing a gasp to her lips.

"I asked you a question," he said.

"Yes. Yes, I like it," Anna panted.

"Hmm," Carter rumbled. He released her hair from his grip and nuzzled down her neck before making his way up to her other ear with kisses.

He growled softly in that ear. "That's not the only question I want answered, young lady. Say you'll marry me now. Every second you make me wait is another hour I'll spend tanning your hide."

Anna waited three long seconds before she said, "I'll marry you, Carter."

Carter smiled and folded her into his arms.

CHAPTER FOURTEEN

The next day, Anna and Carter got married. The only people at the ceremony were the preacher, Paddy, Ben, Grace, and Anna's parents and sisters. Anna didn't wish to have a lavish wedding, preferring to marry right away. As for Carter, he didn't care what the wedding was like, so long as Anna was the bride.

Ben and Grace offered to watch Paddy overnight, so Carter and Anna rode home alone together in the buggy after the ceremony. Their first night as husband and wife stretched before them, full of unknown pleasures and mysteries.

Anna spoke, her voice shy, "I must say you look very handsome, husband." Carter was wearing his Sunday best and had shaved his face, which Anna had told him before that she liked.

He looked at her with awe for the

thousandth time that day. Her hair tumbled in curls and waves around her shoulders. She wore a flowered wreath around her head, her best dress, and white gloves. "Thank you, wife. You're looking rather lovely yourself." He clucked to the horse, eager to get them home.

They reached the cabin, and Carter pulled the brake. He stepped out of the buggy and held his hand out to Anna, which she clasped in her gloved fingers during her descent.

He wrapped his arms around her and pulled her close to him for a kiss. She responded eagerly, her lips parting in a gasp when prodded by his tongue. "I want to taste every part of you," he breathed against her neck. He pulled the shoulder of her dress aside to pepper kisses on her skin. Her head fell back, given him access to her neck, which he nipped gently. "By the end of tonight, you'll never doubt my love for you again."

"I know you love me," she said breathily.

"I'll never let you forget it." Reluctantly, he released her, immediately missing the warmth of her body when it was no longer against him. "Go into the bedroom and wait for me, my love."

It was dusk and would soon be dark. He watched as she moved toward the front door. The white flowers around her wreath caught the light of the moon, making her appear as though she wore a halo. His angel. He couldn't wait to strip her down and defile her.

After attending to the horse and buggy,

Carter entered the cabin and then the bedroom holding a candle. He found Anna sitting on the edge of the bed. Her bare feet dangled just above the floor. Her hair wreath, gloves, shoes, and stockings were piled in the corner, but she still wore her dress. She folded her hands together and focused a wide-eyed gaze at him.

He placed the candle on the dresser. "Anna, do you know how a man and his wife make love?"

"Yes," she said shyly.

He walked to her and cupped her chin, then bent down and kissed her. He would never tire of kissing her. She responded to him in a way that made him want to devour her whole. Slowly, he leaned over her as he kissed her, causing her to lie flat on the bed. His hand wandered down her clothed body. Her breasts, tightly covered except for the cleavage that spilled out, rose under his touch. He had to have her.

Standing up, he took hold of one of her bare ankles and playfully flipped her around to lie on her stomach. She let out a squeal of surprise but made no protest when he leaned over her and unbuttoned the back of her dress, starting at the top.

"I'm looking forward to seeing what's mine under all these layers," he said.

She sighed. "Carter, the things you say. You make me feel so possessed."

"As you should feel. You're mine, and I'm yours. And there are too many buttons on this dress," he added.

Unbuttoning the final one at the bodice, he helped her stand and pull her arms out, then he slipped the dress down and off under her legs. He tossed the dress to the nearest corner, which contained her gloves and stockings. Next, he observed her corset and tried to figure out the fastest way to untie it.

It gripped tightly to her skin, and he couldn't imagine it was comfortable. "You don't usually wear this nonsense, do you?" he asked.

"No, I hate the corset. It's just for church and getting married in."

"I see. I don't see you wearing it after today then. I won't worry too much about ruining it." He untied it and loosened it before gripping the sides and tearing it away from her body.

Anna stood before him, naked from the waist up. "Beautiful," he said, cupping her breasts in his hand and leaning down to kiss them. He took a pert nipple in his mouth, swirling around it with his tongue. She tasted so good, all woman.

"Oh, Carter... I feel so much," she gasped, her knees buckling slightly beneath her.

"Me too, darlin'." He stroked down her side and hooked his thumb in the waist of her petticoat and drawers. He released her breast from his mouth so that he could look at her body as he bared it completely, shimmying her underclothes down until they pooled around her feet at the floor.

Light curls covered her center at the apex of her legs. She stood leaning more on her left foot, causing one hip to jut out suggestively. "You look ravenous, my love."

She smiled in a hazy way that made his heart beat a little faster.

"Lie on the bed," he said.

She stepped back and perched her naked bottom on the edge, then leaned back.

"Not that way. Turn around. I owe you a spanking."

"What? Why?" she protested breathlessly.

"You know why. For running away from me and thinking I didn't love you."

"But... It's our wedding night."

"Turn around, Anna," he said, allowing a hint of sternness to his tone. "Six swats."

She made a noise of protest but then obediently turned so that she bent over the bed, her bare bottom exposed in the air.

For a moment he looked at the back side of her naked body without touching her. She was a sight to behold. Her unbraided tresses spread messily around her shoulders and the quilt. The curve of her shoulders dipped into the small of her back's delicate valley before her bottom rose into a perfect hill.

Carter touched the nape of her neck and stroked along her spine down to her bottom, which he cupped at the curve. He gave it a spank that cracked open the hush in the air. Anna let out a surprised yelp.

"One," he murmured. He rubbed the place he'd just spanked and kissed her shoulder. He didn't want to cause her pain, but he knew a spanking would help her remember how much he cared about her.

He spanked her other cheek and rubbed. "Two." He kissed her opposite shoulder.

Anna's legs parted slightly. He didn't know whether it was an unconscious invitation, but he accepted the offer. He moved his hand to between her legs and fingered her delicate lower lips.

Her legs parted more, opening herself to him, so he stroked her until he felt her juices, which clung to his fingers as he took them away. "You're almost ready for me, my love."

She responded with a moan.

He moved his hand back to her bottom and spanked her again. "Three."

Her back arched, causing her to thrust her bottom harder against his hand. "Oh, Carter. Please touch me again."

Carter meandered back to her sex and found her clit under the soft curls. He brushed the bud with the tips of his fingers and another moan escaped from her lips.

He teased his fingers through the lips of her opening as he moved back toward her bottom, bringing more of her juices with him. A primitive growl escaped from his throat when the scent of her desire found its way to his nose. He spanked her again.

"Four, you naughty girl," he said in a voice low with lust.

"This spanking feels so good."

"*Mmhm.* I can tell that, darlin'. Two more swats. Hard ones you'll never forget."

She threw her head back and raised her luscious bottom to meet his next strokes. He met it with enthusiasm. His hand cracked down hard, once on each cheek.

She kicked up a leg and reached back with both hands to stroke the burn he'd inflicted.

"That's my job," he said, moving her hands aside. He kneaded her reddened cheeks, loving the way her supple skin moved under his touch.

* * *

Anna panted, a churning desire building in her nether regions. She looked back at Carter over her shoulder when he stopped rubbing her bottom. He was unbuttoning his shirt.

"Now you can lie on your back for me, darlin'," he said, locking eyes with her.

She shifted onto her back and perched on her elbows She bent her knees up so that her toes curled over the edge of the bed and closed her knees together, feeling shy.

"No, darlin', keep your legs apart for me."

She allowed her knees to separate while

he shucked off the rest of his clothes. Her gaze traveled down to his cock, fully engorged. She could hardly believe it would fit inside of her, but her mother had assured her that no matter how big it looked, it would fit.

She expected him to lean over her and was surprised when he dropped to his knees and positioned his face between her legs.

"Carter, what are you doing? I thought you were going to make love to me now."

He placed her knees over his shoulders. "This is all part of making love. Do you trust me, Anna? I want to taste you and make you feel things you've never felt."

Anna looked into his eyes and relented with a breathless "I trust you" before collapsing on the bed. She stared at the ceiling, a little embarrassed but mostly aroused and curious.

"Good girl." He breathed heat onto her cleft, sending goosebumps down her arms. When he applied his tongue to her crease and circled around her entrance, she clenched. He probed into her with his tongue, causing the walls of her pussy to contract without satisfaction. His tongue devoured and tortured the inside of her, making her feel desperate.

"Please, Carter," she begged, unsure of what she was begging for. Her legs began to tremble. Carter removed his tongue, which only added to her torment. She shifted onto her elbows to look at him again, her eyes pleading.

"Darling, you taste delicious. I want you."

"I want you too," she said.

"And you shall have me. Tell me, have you ever felt an orgasm by your own hand?"

She blinked. "I don't know."

Carter chuckled. "That means no." He sighed deeply. "Anna, I feel so honored to be your husband and to show you the pleasures of the flesh. I'd like you to try to relax. If I haven't forgotten how to do this, you will soon experience your first orgasm."

"Oh, Carter," she said, lying back and staring at the ceiling again. Every other thing he said to her made her blush.

"I love when my name comes out of your sweet mouth. I want you to yell it when the time comes. Will you do that for me?"

"I will," she vowed, though she didn't know what time was coming exactly.

He dragged his tongue up from her slit to her clit and flicked it, once, twice, three times. He caressed and held it in his lips for a moment before releasing and dancing his tongue around it, letting just the sides of her bud feel pressure. Anna felt overwrought with sensations and grabbed Carter's head, pulling him closer to her center. She heard him groan as he captured her clit again in his lips, applying pressure before releasing. Hungrily, he spiraled around, again and again, prodding and sweeping, nudging her to the brink.

Anna felt something powerful growing from the place Carter had claimed with his mouth.

It built to a climax and her legs shuddered. Carter grabbed her hips in his hands and held her down as she arched her back. He kept her clit enslaved in his lips. A moan erupted from her that turned into a scream. She felt the pressure of his lips on her bud soften, but his hands still held her gyrating hips firmly in place. She writhed until finally the fire in her died down and she collapsed back on the bed.

"Good girl," Carter said, his voice rough. He pushed the back of her thighs with his hands, moving her farther onto the bed, and climbed on top of her. He ensnared a nipple in his mouth and used his skilled tongue to tap it, while his hand and thumb massaged her other breast.

Anna panted. "Carter, everything you do feels so good and so strong."

He released her breast from his mouth and smiled. "I'm glad to hear that. It's about to get stronger yet. Are you ready?"

She suddenly felt awake and at attention. "Are you going to insert now?"

"That is the plan, yes." He chuckled and looked into her eyes. "That was so sweet how you asked that, honey. You are utterly delightful."

Anna wrapped her legs around him and stared back into his eyes.

Carter raised an eyebrow. "Looks like the lady is ready, so I'd better get to it." He pressed the head of his cock into the front of her passage and held it in place for a moment before he plunged slowly but deliberately deep inside of her, rupturing her hymen in one smooth movement. Unfamiliar pain pinched her. She closed her eyes and didn't make a sound while she waited for it to subside. He remained still and quiet until her eyes fluttered open.

When she looked at him, he asked, "All right, my love?"

"Yes," she whispered. She was better than all right. The muscles of her center contracted and gripped him. She now understood why his tongue had been such torture. She needed to feel him inside her like this, stretching and filling her, turning her into a woman whose body was linked to the man she loved.

Carter rocked in and out. She remained still and in awe, paying great mind to what it felt like to be loved in this way. He rode her a little harder and lowered his chest to hers. He spoke in her ear, tickling it. "You're going to come again, and when you do, you're going to obey this time and yell out my name. Is that clear, young lady?"

His words and motions brought the fluttering back to her belly and lit the fire in her sex. "Yes, sir."

He drove into her and commanded her submission to his cock in a way that made her feel weak and powerful at the same time. He enveloped a wrist in each hand and pinned them high above her head, further exerting his domination and possession. She came for the second time that evening and yelled his name.

Carter came shortly after her. He held her to him as the groan broke free from deep inside of him and he spilled his seed inside of her. His motions settled. Rolling onto his back, he brought Anna in his arms with him.

They breathed hard.

Anna rested her head on his chest. She heard his heartbeat against her ear. It was the best, most comforting sound she could have imagined. The man she had grown to love so fiercely was in bed with her, proof of his love and vitality thumping in rhythm against her head.

He stroked her hair. "I love your hair unbraided like this," he said softly.

She could feel her breathing slow. Her eyes felt heavy with sleep, and she was only dimly aware of being moved to rest her head on a pillow. The warmth of his body was still against her. She smiled and curled into her sleeping position.

Carter pulled the quilt up over her. "Sweet dreams, wife," he whispered in her ear, and kissed the back of her neck.

Anna didn't dream. No dream could be sweeter than their time awake together.

The End

BOOKS BY THIS AUTHOR

Bringing Trouble Home

Widowed rancher Heath Wolfe worries he's making a big mistake by bringing Willow McAllister home to his ranch. A known troublemaker around town, she can't seem to keep a job or avoid skirmishes with the law, so the town marshal implores Heath to help. While Heath agrees to employ Willow, he certainly won't allow misbehavior, and he's even prepared to take the willful young lady over his knee for a sound spanking if warranted.

Orphaned and alone for several years, nineteen-year-old Willow is used to taking care of herself. She sleeps wherever she can find a soft surface and roams freely. She doesn't drink whiskey every night and she only steals when she has to, so it doesn't seem fair when the marshal insists she give up her freedom to work for Heath. She suspects that the rancher is as humorless as he is handsome.

Heath and Willow are as different as two people can be, but a tentative friendship forms. Old habits die hard, though, and it doesn't take long for Willow to engage in familiar shenanigans. When problems arise, will Heath regret bringing trouble home, or has Willow finally found a man who can steer her straight?

When He Returns

Proud and independent, thirteen-year-old orphan Wade Hunter doesn't want a family. But when the town marshal catches him stealing, Wade's given only two choices: Spend time in jail or become the marshal's ward.

Sadie Shaw, the marshal's eldest daughter, doesn't want another sibling. She has enough brothers and sisters, and she's dismayed when her kindhearted pa brings home another lost child. It doesn't help that this one is surly and arrogant. Worse, he thinks that because he's older, he's under no obligation to mind her household rules.

Wade and Sadie battle wills often as they grow into adulthood, burgeoning both their dislike for each other and their grudging respect. When faced with a problem that requires their unity, will they be able to set aside their differences, or will the strife they face only tear them apart for good?

Taming Tori

Roughhewn cowboy Frank Bassett knows his life has changed forever after a near-fatal horse accident leaves him with a serious limp. Determined to make the best of his circumstances, he takes a job as a schoolteacher in a small town. There he crosses paths with a beautiful, tart-tongued seamstress, who before long finds herself over his knee to be taught a richly deserved lesson in good manners.

Frank does not fit the bill with regard to Victoria Davis's hope of landing herself a wealthy husband, but the snobby young woman can't resist the magnetic pull of Frank's strength, dominance, and tenderness. She becomes hopelessly smitten, and a tempestuous romance ignites.

But dark clouds loom ahead, and a stroke of misfortune will once again befall the cowboy. Can these two spirited lovers weather the impending storm, or will their love be collateral damage?

Mary Quite Contrary

Nineteen-year-old Mary Appleton manages a successful restaurant in the small town of Thorndale. Though passionate about cooking, she's naïve about the dangers of the world and innocent when it comes to love and romance.

Benjamin Gray, the stern new deputy in town, knows the restaurant is vulnerable to robbers, and his protective instincts ignite when he notices that Mary doesn't safeguard her money. When she refuses to lock up the cash in her register, Deputy Gray gives her only one other choice: Accept a hard spanking over his knee.

To Mary's surprise, the punishment does nothing to quell her attraction to Ben. Rather, she finds herself smitten by her older lover who brings her as much pleasure as pain. But will she accept his advice when it matters most, or will her contrary behavior ruin them both?

Handling Susannah

Rancher Adam Harrington wants to marry a wholesome, virginal bride with a sweet disposition. When he reads a young woman's unusual advertisement requesting a mail-order cowboy as her groom, he thinks they might be a good match, so he writes her a telegram. She pens a favorable response, accepting him as her future husband.

Susannah Smith's father bequeathed his ranch to her, but it was under one condition: She must be married. For Virginia City's fallen woman, finding a man to marry is no easy feat. The men in town who seek to court the hot-tempered, unwed mother are sluggards and drunks, not the kind of men capable of running a ranch. Desperate to find a suitable husband or else lose everything, she expands her search by listing an ad in the paper.

Adam and Susannah meet, and the attraction between them is undeniable, but it is soon followed by wariness. Susannah had planned to marry a man who would do her bidding, not take over everything. It's her ranch, after all. Equally befuddled, Adam thought he'd be marrying a woman who knows her place, not a temperamental brat who could benefit from some time over his knee.

Susannah feels outraged by Adam's authoritative ways, but his dominant handling in the bedroom leaves her trembling with desire. Will she learn to accept his firm leadership and expectations? And will Adam grow to love the woman who differs so drastically from the kind of wife he thought he wanted?

Catching Betsy

Betsy Blake yearns for love and romance, but the unattached men of Virginia City are crude, rough cowboys without the gentlemanly qualities she desires. She pens an advertisement in the paper for a mail-order groom from the east, specifying that he be well-dressed and mannerly.

Roderick Mason's reputation as an architect in New York City has earned him great success, but he hasn't been as lucky in love. The women of his circle are too prim and predictable for the adventurous rake. He longs for excitement and a woman who will challenge him. When he reads Betsy's ad in the paper requesting a gentleman groom, he's intrigued, so he heads west to meet her.

Roderick and Betsy are immediately smitten, but they soon discover that not everyone in Virginia City is pleased by their match, especially one man who wants Betsy as his own. As Betsy's stalker becomes increasingly threatening, Roderick realizes he will go to great lengths to protect his sweet little country girl, including taking her over his knee for some painful discipline when she misbehaves or puts herself in danger. Will Betsy learn to face her problems and accept Roderick's love and discipline, or will he never succeed at what he desires most--protecting and catching Betsy?

Justice For Elsie

Betsy Blake yearns for love and romance, but the

unattached men of Virginia City are crude, rough cowboys without the gentlemanly qualities she desires. She pens an advertisement in the paper for a mail-order groom from the east, specifying that he be well-dressed and mannerly.

Roderick Mason's reputation as an architect in New York City has earned him great success, but he hasn't been as lucky in love. The women of his circle are too prim and predictable for the adventurous rake. He longs for excitement and a woman who will challenge him. When he reads Betsy's ad in the paper requesting a gentleman groom, he's intrigued, so he heads west to meet her.

Roderick and Betsy are immediately smitten, but they soon discover that not everyone in Virginia City is pleased by their match, especially one man who wants Betsy as his own. As Betsy's stalker becomes increasingly threatening, Roderick realizes he will go to great lengths to protect his sweet little country girl, including taking her over his knee for some painful discipline when she misbehaves or puts herself in danger. Will Betsy learn to face her problems and accept Roderick's love and discipline, or will he never succeed at what he desires most--protecting and catching Betsy?

Printed in Great Britain
by Amazon